Enid

Enid Blyton, who died in 1968, is one of the most popular and prolific children's authors of all time. She wrote over seven hundred books which have been translated into many languages throughout the world. She also found time to write numerous songs, poems, and plays, and ran magazines and clubs.

She was always very concerned for the welfare of children in need, and the Enid Blyton Trust, set up after her death, is very active in raising funds for sick and handicapped children.

All eight titles in the Adventure series are available from Piper books:

1. THE ISLAND OF ADVENTURE
2. THE CASTLE OF ADVENTURE
3. THE VALLEY OF ADVENTURE
4. THE SEA OF ADVENTURE
5. THE MOUNTAIN OF ADVENTURE
6. THE SHIP OF ADVENTURE
7. THE CIRCUS OF ADVENTURE
8. THE RIVER OF ADVENTURE

The Castle of Adventure

Enid Blyton

Piper Books

in association with Macmillan Children's Books

First published 1946 by Macmillan and Co Ltd
This revised edition 1988 by Pan Books Ltd,
Cavaye Place, London SW10 9PG
in association with
Macmillan Children's Books Ltd
9 8 7 6

ISBN 0 330 30175 6

Printed and bound in Great Britain by
Richard Clay Ltd, Bungay, Suffolk

Contents

1 Now for the holidays! 7
2 The boys come home – and Kiki! 13
3 Settling in at Spring Cottage 19
4 Tassie and Button 25
5 The way to the castle 30
6 How can they get in? 36
7 Inside the castle of adventure 42
8 Up in the tower 48
9 The eagles' nest 54
10 A curious thing 60
11 An unexpected meeting 66
12 Jack is left at the castle 72
13 Noises in the night 78
14 Jack gets a shock 84
15 The hidden room 90
16 Things begin to happen 96
17 Things go on happening 102
18 Prisoners in the castle 108
19 Lucy-Ann has an idea 114
20 Philip tells a strange story 120
21 Another day goes by 126
22 Tassie is very brave 132
23 A few surprises 138
24 Kiki gives a performance 144
25 At midnight 150
26 Going into hiding 156
27 The adventure boils up 161
28 A terrible storm 168
29 The secret passage 174
30 The other side of the hill 180
31 The end of the castle of adventure 185

1

Now for the holidays!

Two girls sat on a window-seat in their school study. One had red wavy hair, and so many freckles that it was impossible to count them. The other had dark hair that stuck up in front in an amusing tuft.

'One more day and then the hols begin,' said red-haired Lucy-Ann, looking at Dinah out of curious green eyes. 'I'm longing to see Jack again. A whole term is an awfully long time to be away from him.'

'Well, I don't mind being away from *my* brother!' said Dinah, with a laugh. 'Philip's not bad, but he does make me wild, always bringing in those awful animals and insects of his.'

'It's a good thing there's only one day between our breaking-up days,' said Lucy-Ann. 'We shall be home first – and we can have a look round, and then the next day we shall meet the boys – hurrah!'

'I wonder what this place is like, that Mother has taken for the hols,' said Dinah. 'I'll get out her letter and read it again.'

She fished in her pocket for the letter and took it out. She skimmed it through.

'She doesn't say very much. Only that she wants our home to be decorated and cleaned, and so she has taken a cottage somewhere in the hills for us to stay in these hols,' said Dinah. 'Here's the letter.'

Lucy-Ann took it, and read it with interest. 'Yes – it's a place called Spring Cottage, and it's on the side of Castle Hill. She says it's rather a lonely sort of place, but packed with wild birds, so Jack will be very pleased.'

'I can't understand your brother being so mad on birds,' said Dinah. 'He's just as bad about birds as Philip is about insects and animals.'

'Philip is marvellous with animals, I think,' said Lucy-Ann, who had a great admiration for Dinah's brother. 'Do you remember that mouse he trained to take crumbs from between his teeth?'

'Oh, don't remind me of those things!' said Dinah, with a shudder. She could not bear even a spider near her, and bats and mice made her squeal. Lucy-Ann thought it was amazing that she should have lived so many years with an animal-loving boy like Philip, and yet still be afraid of things.

'He does tease you, doesn't he?' she said to Dinah, remembering how Philip had often put earwigs under Dinah's pillow, and black beetles in her shoes. He really was a terrible tease when he was in the mood. No wonder Dinah had such a temper!

'I wonder how Kiki has got on this term,' said Dinah.

Kiki was Jack's parrot, an extremely clever bird, who could imitate voices and sounds in a most remarkable manner. Jack had taught her many phrases, but Kiki had picked up many many more herself, especially from a cross old uncle that Lucy-Ann and Jack had once lived with.

'Kiki wasn't going to be allowed to be at school with Jack this term,' said Lucy-Ann sadly. 'It's an awful pity – but still he got a friend in the town to look after her for him, and he goes to see her every day. But I do think they might have let him have her at school.'

'Well, considering that Kiki kept telling the headmaster not to sniff, and Jack's form master to wipe his feet, and woke everyone up at night by screeching like a railway engine, I'm not surprised they didn't want Kiki this term,' said Dinah. 'Anyway, we'll be able to have her for the hols and that will be nice. I really do like Kiki – she doesn't seem like a bird, but like one of us, somehow.'

Kiki certainly was a good companion. Although she didn't converse with the children properly, she could talk nineteen to the dozen when she wanted to, saying the most ridiculous things and making the children laugh till they cried. She adored Jack, and would sit quietly on his shoulder for hours if he would let her.

The girls were glad that the holidays were so soon coming. They and the two boys and Kiki would have good fun together. Lucy-Ann especially looked forward to being with Dinah's pretty, merry mother.

Jack and Lucy-Ann Trent had no father or mother, and had lived with a cross old uncle for years, until by chance they had met Philip and Dinah Mannering. These two had no father, but they had a mother, who worked hard for them. She worked so hard that she had no time to make a home for them, so they were sent to boarding school, and in the holidays went to an aunt and uncle.

But now things were changed. Dinah's mother had enough money to make a home for them, and had offered to have their great friends, Jack and Lucy-Ann, as well. So in term time the two girls went to school together, and the two boys were at another school. In the holidays all four joined up with Mrs Mannering, the mother of Philip and Dinah.

'No more uncles and aunts!' said Dinah joyfully, who hadn't much liked her absent-minded old Uncle Jocelyn. 'Just a lovely home with my mother!'

Now, in the coming holidays, they were all to be together in this holiday cottage that Mrs Mannering had found. Although Dinah was a little disappointed at not going back to the home her mother had made for them all, she couldn't help looking forward to the holiday cottage. It sounded nice – and what fine walks and picnics they would have among the hills!

'Do you remember that marvellous adventure we had last summer?' she said to Lucy-Ann, who was looking dreamily out of the window, thinking how lovely it would be to see her brother Jack the day after next.

Lucy-Ann nodded. 'Yes,' she said, and she screwed up her freckled nose a little. 'It was the most exciting adventure anyone could have – but oh dear, how afraid I was sometimes! That Isle of Gloom – do you remember it, Dinah?'

'Yes – and that shaft going right down into the heart of the earth – and how we got lost there – golly, that *was* an adventure!' said Dinah. 'I wouldn't mind having another one, really.'

'You *are* funny!' said Lucy-Ann. 'You shiver and shake when you see a spider, but yet you seem to enjoy adventures so exciting that they make me tremble even to remember them!'

'Well – we shan't have any more,' said Dinah, rather regretfully. 'One adventure like that is enough for a lifetime, I suppose. I bet the boys will want to talk about it again and again. Do you remember how in the Christmas hols we couldn't make them stop?'

'Oh – I wish the hols would come quickly!' said Lucy-Ann, getting off the window-seat restlessly. 'I don't know why these last two or three days always drag so.'

But tomorrow came at last, and the two girls went off in the train with scores of their friends, chattering and laughing. Their luggage was safely in the van, their tickets were in their purses, their hearts beat fast in delight. Now for the holidays!

They had to change trains twice, but Dinah was good at that sort of thing. Lucy-Ann was timid and shy in her dealings with strangers, but twelve-year-old Dinah stood no nonsense from anyone. She was a strapping, confident girl, well able to hold her own. Lucy-Ann seemed two or three years younger to Dinah, although actually there was only one year between them.

At last they were at the station for their holiday home.

They leapt out and Dinah found the one and only porter. He went to get their luggage.

'There's Mother!' shouted Dinah, and rushed to her pretty, bright-eyed mother, who had come to meet them. Dinah was not one to hug or kiss very much, but Lucy-Ann made up for that! Dinah gave her mother one quick peck of a kiss, but Lucy-Ann gave her a bear-hug, and rubbed her red head happily against Mrs Mannering's chin.

'Oh, it's lovely to see you again!' she said, thinking for the hundredth time how lucky Dinah was to have a mother of her own. She felt grateful to her for letting her share her. It wasn't very nice, having no father or mother to write to you, or welcome you home. But Mrs Mannering always made her feel that she loved her and wanted her.

'I've got the car outside to meet you,' said Mrs Mannering. 'Come along. The porter will bring your luggage.'

They went out of the station. It was only a little country station. Outside was a country lane, its banks starred with spring flowers. The sky was blue and the air was warm and soft. Lucy-Ann felt very happy. It was the first day of the holidays, she was with Dinah's lovely mother, and tomorrow the boys came home.

They got into the little car, and the porter put the trunks in at the back. Mrs Mannering took the wheel.

'It's quite a long way to Spring Cottage,' she said. 'We have to fetch our own goods and food from the village here, except for eggs and butter and milk which a nearby farm lets me have. But it's lovely country, and there are marvellous walks for you. As for birds – well, Jack will have the time of his life!'

'It's nesting time too – he'll be thinking of nothing but eggs and nests,' said Lucy-Ann, feeling just a little jealous of the bird life that took up so much of her brother's time.

The girls looked round them as Mrs Mannering drove along. It certainly was lovely country. It was very hilly, and in the distance the hills looked blue and rather exciting. The car ran along a road down a winding river valley, and then began to climb a steep hill.

'Oh, is our cottage on the side of this hill?' asked Dinah, thrilled. 'What a lovely view we'll have Mother!'

'We have – right across the valley to other hills, and yet more hills rising beyond them!' said her mother. The car had to go very slowly now, for the road was steep. As they rose higher and higher, the girls could see more and more across the valley. Then Lucy-Ann glanced upwards to see how high they were – and she gave a shout.

'I say! Look at that castle on the top of the hill! Just look at it!'

Dinah looked. It certainly was a most imposing and rugged old castle. It had a tower at each end, and its walls looked thick. It had slit windows – but it had wide ones too, which looked a little odd.

'Is it a really old castle?' asked Lucy-Ann.

'No – not really,' said Mrs Mannering. 'Some of it is old, but most of it has been restored and rebuilt, so that it is a real mix-up. Nobody lives there now. I don't know who it belongs to, either – no one seems to know or care. It's shut up, and hasn't a very good name.'

'Why? Did something horrid happen there once?' asked Dinah, feeling rather thrilled.

'I think so,' said her mother. 'But I really don't know anything about it. You'd better not go up there, anyhow, because the road up to it has had a landslide or something, and is very dangerous. They say that part of the castle is ready to slip down the hill!'

'Gracious! I hope it won't slip on to our cottage!' said Lucy-Ann, half scared.

Mrs Mannering laughed. 'Of course not. We are nowhere near it – look, there's our cottage, tucked away among those trees.'

It was a lovely little cottage, with a thatched roof and small leaded windows. The girls loved it the minute they saw it.

'It's just a bit like the house you bought for us,' said Dinah. 'That's pretty too. Oh, Mother, we shall have a lovely time here! Won't the boys be thrilled?'

There was a fair-sized shed at the side into which Mrs Mannering drove the car. Everyone got out. 'Leave the trunks for a bit,' said Dinah's mother. 'The man who comes from the farm will carry them in. Now – welcome to Spring Cottage!'

2

The boys come home – and Kiki!

That day and the morning of the next the two girls spent in exploring their holiday home. It was certainly a tiny place, but just big enough for them. There was a large old fashioned kitchen and a tiny parlour. Above were three small bedrooms.

'One for Mother, one for you and me, Lucy-Ann, and one for the boys,' said Dinah. 'Mother's going to do the cooking and we're all to help with the housework, which won't be much. Isn't our bedroom sweet?'

It was a little room tucked into the thatched roof, with a window jutting out from the thatch. The walls slanted in an odd fashion, and the ceiling slanted too. The floor was very uneven, and the doorways were low, so that Dinah who was growing tall, had to lower her head under one or two in case she bumped it.

'Spring Cottage,' she said. 'It's a nice name for it, especially in the springtime.'

'It's named because of the spring that runs down behind it,' said her mother. 'The water starts somewhere up in the yard of the castle, I believe, runs down through a tunnel it has made for itself, and gushes out just above the cottage at the back. It runs through the garden then, and disappears down the hillside.'

The girls explored the spring. They found where it gushed out, and Dinah tasted the water. It was cold and crystal clear. She liked hearing the gurgling sound it made in the untidy little garden. She heard it all night long in her sleep and loved it.

The view from the cottage was magnificent. They could see the whole of the valley below, and could follow too the winding road that led up to their cottage. Far away in the distance was the railway station, looking like a toy building. Twice a day a train came into it, and it too looked like a toy.

'Just like the railway engine and carriages that Jack used to have,' said Lucy-Ann, remembering. 'And how cross our old Uncle Geoffrey was when we used to set it going! He said it made more noise than a thunderstorm. Golly, I'm glad we don't live with him any more.'

Dinah looked at her watch. 'It's almost time to meet the train,' she said. 'I bet the boys are feeling excited! Come on. Let's find my mother.'

Mrs Mannering was just about to go and get the car out. The girls packed themselves in beside her. Lucy-Ann felt terribly excited. She was so looking forward to being with Jack again. And with Philip too. It would be lovely to be all together once more. She did hope Dinah wouldn't fly into one of her tempers *too* soon! She and Philip quarrelled far too much.

They arrived at the little station. The train was not yet signalled. Lucy-Ann walked up and down, longing to see the signal go down – and then, with an alarming clank, it did go down. Almost at the same moment the smoke of the train appeared, and then, round the corner, came the engine, puffing vigorously, for it was uphill to the station.

Both the boys were hanging out of the window, waving and shouting. The girls screamed greetings, and capered about in delight.

'There's Kiki!' shouted Lucy-Ann. 'Kiki! Good old Kiki!'

With a screech Kiki flew off Jack's shoulder and landed on Lucy-Ann's. She rubbed her beak against the little girl's cheek and made a curious cracking noise. She was delighted to see her.

The boys jumped out of the carriage. Jack rushed to Lucy-Ann and gave her a hug which the little girl returned, her eyes shining. Kiki gave another screech and flew back on to Jack's shoulder.

'Wipe your feet,' she said sternly to the startled porter. 'And where is your handkerchief?'

Philip grinned at his sister Dinah. 'Hallo, old thing,' he said. 'You've grown! Good thing I have too, or you'd be as tall as I am! Hallo, Lucy-Ann – *you* haven't grown! Been a good girl at school?'

'Don't talk like a grown-up!' said Dinah. 'Mother's outside in the car. Come and see her.'

The porter took their trunks on his barrow and followed the four excited children. Kiki flew down to the barrow and looked at him with bright eyes.

'How many times have I told you to shut the door?' she said. The porter dropped the handles of the barrow in surprise. He didn't know whether to answer this extraordinary bird or not.

Kiki gave a laugh just like Jack's and flew out to the car. She joined the others, and tried to get on to Mrs Mannering's shoulder. She liked Dinah's mother very much.

'Attention, please,' said Kiki sternly. 'Open your books at page six.'

Everyone laughed. 'She got that from one of the masters,'

said Jack. 'Oh, Aunt Allie, she was so funny in the train. She put her head out of the window at every station and said "Right away, there!" just as she had heard a guard say, and you should have seen the engine-driver's face!'

'It's lovely to have you back,' said Lucy-Ann, keeping close to Jack. She adored her brother though he didn't really take a great deal of notice of her. They all got into the car, and the porter shoved the luggage in somehow, keeping a sharp eye on Kiki.

'Please shut the door,' she said, and went off into one of her never-ending giggles.

'Shut up, Kiki,' said Jack, seeing the porter's startled face. 'Behave yourself, or I'll send you back to school.'

'Oh, you naughty boy!' said Kiki; 'oh, you naughty, naughty, naughty . . .'

'I'll put an elastic band round your beak if you dare to say another word!' said Jack. 'Can't you see I want to talk to Aunt Allie?'

Jack and Lucy-Ann called Mrs Mannering Aunt Allie, because 'Mrs Mannering' seemed too stiff and standoffish. She liked both children very much, but especially Lucy-Ann, who was far more gentle and affectionate than Dinah had ever been.

'I say – this looks exciting country!' said Philip, looking out of the car windows. 'Plenty of birds here for you, Freckles – and plenty of animals for me!'

'Where's that brown rat you had this term?' said Jack, with a mischievous glance at Dinah. She gave a squeal at once.

Philip began to feel about in his pockets, diving into first one and then the other, whilst Dinah watched him in horror, expecting to see a brown rat appear at any moment.

'Mother! Stop the car and let me walk!' begged Dinah. 'Philip's got a rat somewhere on him.'

'Here he is – no, it's my hanky,' said Philip. 'Ah – what's

this? – no, that's not him. Now – here we are . . . .'

He pretended to be trying to get something out of his pocket with great difficulty. 'Ah, you'd bite, would you?'

Dinah squealed again, and her mother stopped the car. Dinah fumbled at the door-handle.

'No, you stay in, Dinah,' said her mother. 'Philip, you get out and the rat too. I quite agree with Dinah – there are to be no rats running all over us. So you can get out and walk, Philip.'

'Well, Mother – as a matter of fact – I've left the rat behind at school,' said Philip, with a grin. 'I was just teasing Dinah, that's all.'

'Beast!' said Dinah.

'I thought you were,' said his mother, driving on again. 'Well, you nearly had to walk home, so just be careful! I don't mind any of your creatures myself, except rats or snakes. Now, what do you think of Spring Cottage?'

The boys liked it just as much as the girls did – but it was the strange old castle that really took their fancy. Dinah forgot to sulk as she pointed it out to the boys.

'We'll go up there,' said Jack, at once.

'I think not,' said Mrs Mannering. 'I've just explained to the girls that it's dangerous up there.'

'Oh – but why?' asked Jack, disappointed.

'Well, there has been a landslide on the road, and no one dares to set foot on it now,' said Mrs Mannering. 'I did hear that the whole castle is slipping a bit, and might collapse if the road crumbles much more.'

'It sounds very exciting,' said Philip, his eyes gleaming.

They went indoors and the girls showed them their room up in the roof. Lucy-Ann was so delighted to be with Jack that she could hardly leave him for a minute. He was very like her, with deep-red hair, green eyes and hundreds of freckles. He was a very natural, kindly boy, and most people liked him at once.

Philip, whom Jack often called Tufty, was very like *his* sister too, but much more even-tempered. He had the same unruly lock of hair in front, and even their mother had this, so that Jack often referred to them as 'The Three Tufties.' The boys were older than the two girls, and very good friends indeed.

'Holidays at last!' said Philip, undoing his trunk. Dinah watched him from a safe distance.

'Got any creatures in there?' she asked.

'Only a baby hedgehog; and you needn't worry, he's got no fleas,' said Philip.

'I bet he has,' said Dinah, moving a few steps back. 'I shan't forget that hedgehog you found last summer.'

'I tell you, this baby one hasn't got any fleas at all,' said Philip. 'I got some stuff from the chemist and powdered him well, and he's as clean as can be. His spines haven't turned brown yet!'

The girls looked with interest as Philip showed them a tiny prickly ball rolled up in his jerseys in the trunk. It uncurled a little and showed a tiny snout.

'He's sweet,' said Lucy-Ann, and even Dinah didn't mind him.

'The only snag about him is – he's going to be awfully prickly to carry about with me,' said Philip, putting the tiny thing into his shorts pocket.

'You'll probably stop carrying him about when you've sat on him once or twice,' said Dinah.

'I probably shall,' said Philip. 'And just see you don't annoy me too much, Di – for he'd be a marvellous thing to put into your bed!'

'Shut up bickering, you two, and let's go out and explore,' said Jack. 'Lucy-Ann says there's a spring in the garden that comes all the way down from the castle.'

'I'm king of the castle,' said Kiki, swaying gently to and fro on top of the dressing-table. 'Pop goes the weasel.'

'You're getting a bit mixed,' said Jack. 'Come on – out we all go!'

3

Settling in at Spring Cottage

The first day or two were very happy days indeed. The four children and Kiki wandered about as they pleased, and Jack found so many hundreds of nests that he marvelled to see them. He was mad on birds, and would spend hours watching them, if the others let him.

He got very excited one day because he said he saw an eagle. 'An *eagle*!' said Dinah disbelievingly. 'Why, I thought eagles were extinct, and couldn't be found any more – like that Great Auk you always used to be talking about.'

'Well, eagles aren't extinct, said Jack scornfully. 'That just shows how little you know. I'm sure this was an eagle. It soared up and up and up into the air just as eagles are said to do. I believe it was a Golden Eagle.'

'Is it dangerous?' said Dinah.

'Well, I suppose it might attack you if you went too near its nest,' said Jack, 'Golly – I wonder if it *is* nesting anywhere near here!'

'Well, I'm not going eagle-nesting,' said Dinah firmly. 'Anyway, Jack, you've found about a hundred nests already – surely that's enough for you without wanting to see an eagle's nest as well.'

Jack never took birds' eggs, nor did he disturb the sitting birds at all. No bird was ever afraid of him, any more than any animal was ever afraid of Philip. If Lucy or Dinah so much as looked at a nest, the sitting bird seemed frightened and flew off – but she would allow Jack to stroke her, without moving a feather! It was very odd.

Kiki always came with them on their excursions, sitting on Jack's shoulder. He had taught her not to make a sound when he wanted to watch any bird, but Kiki seemed to object to the rooks that lived around. There was a large rookery in one clump of trees not far off, and Kiki would often go to sit on a nearby branch and address rude remarks to the astonished rooks.

'It's a pity they can't answer her back,' said Philip. 'But all they say is "Caw-caw-caw." '

'Yes, and Kiki says it too, now,' said Jack. 'She goes on cawing for ages unless I stop her. Don't you, Kiki?'

Kiki took Jack's ear into her sharp curved beak and fondled it gently. She loved Jack to talk to her. She made a cracking noise with her beak, and said lovingly, 'Caw-caw-caw-caw-caw . . .'

'All right, that's enough,' said Jack. 'Go and listen to a nightingale or something and imitate that! A rook's caw isn't anything to marvel at. Stop, Kiki!'

Kiki stopped, and gave a realistic sneeze. 'Where's your hanky, where's your hanky?' she said.

To Lucy-Ann's delight, Jack gave her a hanky, and Kiki spent the next minute or two holding it in her clawed foot and dabbing her beak with it, sniffing all the time.

'New trick,' explained Jack, with a grin. 'Good, isn't it?'

There were gorgeous walks around the cottage. It was about three miles to the little village, and except for the few houses and the one general shop there, there were no other houses save for a farm or two, and a lonely farm cottage here and there in the hills.

'We're not likely to have any adventures *here*,' said Philip. 'It's all so quiet and peaceful. The village folk have hardly a word to say, have they? They say "Ah, that's right" to everything.'

'They're amazed by Kiki,' said Dinah.

'Ah, that's right,' said Jack, imitating the speech of the villagers.

Kiki immediately did the same. 'Do you remember when Kiki got locked up in a cave underground, and the man who locked her up heard her talking to herself, and thought she was me?' said Jack, remembering the adventure of the summer before. 'My word, that was an adventure!'

'I'd like another adventure, really,' said Philip. 'But I don't expect we'll have another all our lives long.'

'Well, they say adventures come to the adventurous,' said Jack. 'And we're pretty adventurous, I think. I don't see why we shouldn't have plenty more.'

'I wish we could go up and explore that strange castle,' said Dinah longingly, looking up to where it towered on the summit of the hill. 'It looks such an odd place, so deserted and lonely, standing up there, frowning over the valley. Mother says something horrid once happened there, but she doesn't know what.'

'We'll try and find out,' said Jack promptly. He always liked hair-raising tales. 'I expect people were killed there, or something.'

'Oooh, how horrid – I don't want to go up there,' said Lucy-Ann at once.

'Well, Mother said we weren't to, anyhow,' said Dinah.

'She might let us go eagle-nesting,' said Philip. 'And if our search took us near the castle, we couldn't very well help it, could we?'

'We'd better tell her, if we do go anywhere near,' said Jack, who didn't like the idea of deceiving Philip's kindly mother in any way. 'I'll ask her if she minds.'

So he asked her that evening. 'Aunt Allie, I believe there may be an eagle's nest somewhere on the top of this hill,' he said. 'It's so high it's almost a mountain – and that's where eagles nest, you know. You wouldn't mind if I tried to find the nest, would you?'

'No, not if you are careful,' said Mrs Mannering. 'But would your hunt take you anywhere near the old castle?'

'Well, it might,' said Jack honestly. 'But you can trust us not to fool about on any landslides, Aunt Allie. We shouldn't dream of getting the girls into danger.'

'Apparently there was a cloudburst on the top of this hill some years back,' said Mrs Mannering, 'and such a deluge of water fell that it undermined the foundations of the castle, and most of the road up to it slid away down the hillside. So, you see, it really might be very dangerous to explore up there.'

'We'll be very careful,' promised Jack, delighted that Mrs Mannering hadn't forbidden outright their going up the hill to the castle.

He told the others, and they were thrilled. 'We'll go up tomorrow, shall we?' said Jack. 'I really do want to hunt about to see if there is any sign of an eagle's nest.'

That afternoon, in their wanderings, they had a curious feeling of being followed. Once or twice Jack turned round, sure that someone was behind them. But there was never anyone there.

'Funny,' he said to Philip in a low voice. 'I felt certain there was someone behind us then – I heard the crack of a twig – as if someone had trodden on it and broken it.'

'Yes – I thought so too,' said Philip. He looked puzzled. 'I tell you what, Jack. When we get into that patch of trees, I'll crouch down behind a bush and stop, whilst you others go on. Then, if there's anyone following behind us for some reason, I'll see them.'

The girls were told what Philip was going to do. They too had felt that there was someone behind them. They all walked into the patch of trees, and then, when he came to a conveniently thick bush, Philip dropped down suddenly behind it and hid, whilst the others walked on, talking loudly.

Philip lay there and listened. He could hear nothing at first. Then he heard a rustle and his heart beat fast. Who *was* it tracking them, and why? There didn't seem any sense in it.

Someone came up to his bush. Someone crept past without seeing him. Philip gazed at the Someone and was so astonished that he let out an exclamation.

'*Well!*'

A girl with ragged clothes, bare feet and wild, curling hair, jumped violently and turned round. In a trice Philip had jumped up and had hold of her wrists. He did not hold her roughly, but he held her too firmly for her to get away. She tried to bite him, and kicked out with her bare feet.

'Now don't be silly,' said Philip. 'I'll let you go when you tell me who you are and why you are following us.'

The girl said nothing, but glared at Philip out of black eyes. The others, hearing Philip's voice, came running back.

'This is the person who was following us, but I can't get a word out of her,' said Philip.

'She's a wild girl,' said Dinah. The girl scowled at her. Then she glanced at Kiki, on Jack's shoulder, and stared as if she couldn't take her eyes off her.

'I believe she was only following us to get a glimpse of the parrot!' said Philip, with a laugh. 'Is that right, wild girl?'

The girl nodded, 'Ah, that's right,' she said.

'Ah, that's right,' said Kiki. The girl stared and gave a laugh of surpise. It altered her face at once, and gave her a merry, mischievous look.

'What's your name?' asked Philip, letting go her wrists.

'Tassie,' said the girl. 'I saw that bird, and I came after you. I didn't mean no harm. I live round the hill with my mother. I know where you live. I know all you do.'

'Oh – been spying round a bit, and following us, I suppose!' said Jack. 'Do you know this hillside well?'

Tassie nodded. Her bright black eyes hardly left Kiki. She seemed fascinated by the parrot.

'Pop goes the weasel,' said Kiki to her, in a solemn voice. 'Open your book at page six.'

'I say – do you know if the eagles nest on this hill?' asked Jack suddenly. He thought it quite likely that this wild little girl might know things like that.

'What's an eagle?' said Tassie.

'A big bird,' said Jack. 'A very big bird with a curved beak, and . . .'

'Like your bird there?' said Tassie, pointing to Kiki.

'Oh no,' said Jack. 'Well – never mind. If you don't know what an eagle is like, you won't know where it nests either.'

'It's time to go back home,' said Philip. 'I'm hungry. Tassie, take us the shortest way home!'

To Philip's surprise Tassie turned round and plunged down the hillside, as sure-footed as a goat. The others followed. She took them such a short cut that all of them were amazed when they saw Spring Cottage in front of them.

'Thanks, Tassie,' said Philip, and Kiki echoed his words. 'Thanks, Tassie.'

Tassie smiled, and her usual, rather sulky look fled. 'I'll see you again,' she said, and turned to go.

'Did you say you lived at that old cottage round the hill?' yelled Jack after her.

'Ah, that's right!' she shouted back, and disappeared into the bushes.

4

Tassie and Button

Certainly Castle Hill was a very lonely place, for, after they had explored it, there seemed to be only their cottage on it, Tassie's tumble-down home, and a farm some way off, where they got their eggs and milk. The village lay in the valley below.

But although the great hill was almost empty of people, it was full of wild life: birds for Jack, and animals of all kinds for Philip. Squirrels ran everywhere, rabbits popped up wherever they walked, and red foxes slunk by, not seeming at all scared.

'Golly! I wish I could get a baby fox, a little cub!' said Philip. 'I've always wanted one. They're like small and lively puppies, you know.'

Tassie was with them when he said this. She often joined up with them now, and was quite invaluable because she always knew the way home. It seemed very easy to get lost on the vast hill, but Tassie could always show them a short cut.

She was an odd girl. Sometimes she would not come near them but hovered about, some yards off, looking at Kiki with fascinated eyes. Sometimes she walked close to them, and listened to their talk, though she never said very much herself.

She looked with admiration and envy on the simple clothes of the two girls. Sometimes she took the stuff they were made of between her fingers and felt it. She never wore anything but a ragged frock that looked as if it had been made from a dirty sack. Her wild, curly hair was in a tangle, and she was always barefoot.

'I don't mind her being barefoot, but she's rather dirty,' said Lucy-Ann to Dinah. 'I don't believe she ever has a bath.'

'Well, she's probably not seen a bath in her life,' said Dinah. 'She looks awfully healthy though, doesn't she? I've never seen anyone with such bright eyes and pink cheeks and white teeth. Yet I bet she never cleans her teeth.'

On enquiry, it was found that Tassie didn't know what a bath was. Dinah took her into Spring Cottage and showed her the big tin bath they all used. Her mother was there and looked at the wild girl in amazement.

'Whoever is that dirty little girl?' she asked Lucy-Ann in a low voice. 'She'd better have a bath.'

Lucy-Ann knew Mrs Mannering would say that. Mothers thought a lot about people being clean. But when Dinah explained to Tassie what having a bath meant, Tassie looked scared. She shrank back in horror at the thought of sitting down in water.

'Now you listen to me,' said Mrs Mannering firmly. 'If you like to let me give you a bath and scrub you well, I'll find a cotton frock of Dinah's for you, and a ribbon for your hair.'

The thought of this finery thrilled Tassie to such an extent that she consented to have a bath. So she was shut up in the kitchen with Dinah's mother, a bath of hot water and plenty of soap.

After a bit such agonised shrieks came from the kitchen that the children in the garden outside wondered what could be happening. Then they heard Mrs Mannering's firm voice.

'Sit down properly. Get wet all over. Now don't be silly, Tassie. Think of that pretty blue cotton frock over there.'

More shrieks. Evidently Tassie had sat down but didn't like it. There came the sound of scrubbing.

'Your mother's doing the job thoroughly,' said Jack, with a grin. 'Pooh, what a smell of carbolic!'

In half an hour's time Tassie came out of the kitchen,

looking quite different. Her tanned face and arms were now only dark with sunburn, not with dirt. Her hair was washed and brushed, and tied back with a blue ribbon. She wore a blue cotton frock of Dinah's and on her feet she actually had a pair of old rubber shoes!

'Oh, Tassie – you look fine!' said Lucy-Ann, and Tassie looked pleased. She fancied herself very much indeed in her new clothes, and kept stroking the blue frock as if it was a cat.

'I smell nice,' she said, evidently liking the smell of carbolic soap better than the others did. 'But that bath was dreadful. How often do you have a bath? Once a year?'

Tassie was extraordinary. She could not read or write, and yet, like a Red Indian, she could read the signs in the woods and fields in a way that really astonished the children. She was more like a very intelligent animal than a little girl. She attached herself to Philip and also to Kiki, and plainly thought that he and the parrot were the most admirable members of the party.

The day after her bath, she came down to the cottage and looked in at the window. She held something in her arms and the others wondered what it was.

'There's Tassie,' said Lucy-Ann. 'She's got her blue frock on. But her hair's all in a tangle again. And whatever has she got round her neck?'

'Her shoes!' said Philip with a grin. 'I knew she wouldn't wear *those* long! She's so used to being barefooted that shoes would hurt her. But she can't bear to part with them, so she's strung them round her neck.'

'What *has* she got in her arms?' said Dinah curiously. 'Tassie, come in and show us what you've got.'

Tassie grinned, showing all her even white teeth, and went round to the back door. She appeared in the kitchen, and Philip gave a yell.

'It's a fox-cub! Oh, the pretty little thing! Tassie, where *did* you get it?'

'From its den,' said Tassie. 'I knew where a fox family lived, you see.'

Philip took the little cub in his arms. It was the prettiest thing imaginable, with its sharp little nose, its small brush-tail and its thick red coat. It lay quivering in Philip's arms, looking up at him.

Before many seconds had passed the spell that Philip seemed to put on all animals fell upon the fox cub. It crept up to his neck and licked him. It cuddled against him. It showed him in every way it could that it loved him.

'You've got a wonderful way with animals,' said his mother. 'Just like your father had. What a dear little cub, Philip! Where are you going to keep it? You will have to keep it in some sort of cage, won't you, or it will run off.'

'Of course not, Mother!' said Philip scornfully. 'I shall train it to run to heel, like a puppy. It will soon learn.'

'Well, but foxes are such wild creatures,' said his mother doubtfully. But no creature was wild with Philip. Before two hours had gone by the cub was scampering at Philip's heels, begging to be taken into his arms whenever the boy stopped.

Philip's liking for the little wild girl increased very much after that. He found that she knew an amazing amount about animals and their ways.

'She's like Philip's dog, always following him about,' said Dinah. 'Fancy anyone wanting to follow Philip!'

Dinah was not feeling very fond of her brother at that moment. He had four beetles just then, which he said he was training to be obedient to certain commands. He kept them in his bedroom, but they wandered about in a manner that was most terrifying to poor Dinah.

Kiki disliked Philip's fox cub very much and scolded it vigorously whenever she saw it. But Tassie she loved, and flew to her shoulder as soon as she saw her, murmuring nonsense into her ear. Tassie, of course, was delighted about this, and felt enormously proud when Kiki came to her.

'You may think Tassie simply adores you but you come second to Kiki, all the same!' Dinah told Philip with a laugh.

'I wish Kiki would leave Button alone,' said Philip. Button was the name he had given to the little fox-cub, which, like Tassie, followed him about whenever it could. 'Kiki is really behaving badly about Button. I suppose she's jealous.'

'How many times have I told you to wipe your feet?' Kiki demanded of Button. 'Where's your handkerchief? God save the weasel! Pop goes the Queen!'

The children yelled with laughter. It was always funny when Kiki got mixed up in her sentences. Kiki regarded them solemnly, head on one side.

'Attention, please! Open your book at page six.'

'Shut up, Kiki! You remind me of school!' said Jack. 'I say, you others – I saw that eagle again today. It was soaring over the hill-top, and its wing spread was terrific. I'm sure it's got a nest up there.'

'Well, let's go up and find it,' said Dinah. 'I'm longing to have a squint at that old castle, anyway. Even if we can't go up the road that has landslided – or is it landslid? – we can get as close to it as possible and see what it's like.'

'Yes – let's do something exciting,' said Lucy-Ann. 'Let's take our tea out, and go up the hill as far as we can. You can look for eagles' nests, Jack, and we'll have a look at the old castle. It looks so strange and mysterious up there, frowning down at the valley, as if it had some secret to hide.'

'It's empty, you know,' said Philip. 'Probably full of mice and spiders and bats, but otherwise empty.'

'Oooh, don't let's go inside then,' said Dinah at once. 'I'd rather find an eagle's nest than get mixed up with bats inside the old castle!'

5

The way to the castle

'We're going up to the top of the hill, Mother,' said Philip. 'Hunting for an eagle's nest, to please old Jack. He's seen that eagle again. We won't go up the road, so you needn't worry – the road to the castle, I mean.'

'Take your tea with you,' said his mother. 'I shall be glad to be rid of you all for the afternoon! I can do some reading for a change!'

She and Dinah cut sandwiches, and packed up cake and fruit and milk. Philip took the knapsack with the food, and whistled to Button, who now answered his name or a whistle for all the world as if he were a dog.

Button came running to him, giving little sharp barks. He was a most attractive cub and even Mrs Mannering liked him, though she said he smelt a bit strong sometimes. She objected to Button sleeping on Philip's bed, and she and Philip had lengthy arguments about this.

'Your bedroom's full of all kinds of creatures already,' she said. 'There's that hedgehog always in and out of your room now – and yesterday there was something jumping about all over the place.'

Dinah shuddered. She never went into Philip's room if she could help it.

'It was only old Terence the Toad,' said Philip. 'I've got him somewhere about me now, so he won't be leaping about in my bedroom. I'll show him to you – he's got the most beautiful eyes you ever . . .'

'No, Philip,' said his mother firmly. 'I don't want to see him. Don't disturb him.'

Philip stopped ferreting about his person, and put on an

injured expression. 'Nobody ever . . .' he began, but Button took his attention by trying to climb up his leg to get into his arms. 'What's the matter, Button? Has Kiki been teasing you again? Has she been pulling your tail?'

The fox cub chattered to him, and finally settled down comfortably on the top of the knapsack which Philip had slung across his back. 'Where are the others?' said Philip. 'Oh, there they are. Hi, everyone, are you ready?'

They set off up the winding roadway, narrow and steep, just wide enough to take a cart. Tassie soon appeared from somewhere, still wearing the cotton frock, though it was now torn and dirty. She had the rubber shoes tied round her waist that day. It amused the children that she always brought them with her, although she never wore them.

'Her feet must be as hard as nails,' said Jack. 'She never seems to mind treading on the sharpest stones!'

Tassie attached herself to Philip and Button. Kiki addressed a few amiable remarks to her, and then flew off over the rookery to startle the rooks with her realistic cawings. They could never get over their astonishment at this performance, and listened in silence until Kiki talked like a human being, when they all flew away in disgust.

The children went on up the road. It was very hot that afternoon, and they panted and puffed as they climbed. 'Why did we choose an afternoon like this to go up to the castle?' said Philip.

Tassie stopped. 'To the castle?' she said. 'You can't go this way. The road up above is blocked. You can only get round the back now.'

'Well, we want to see what there is to be seen,' said Philip. 'I'd like to see this landslide or whatever it is. We won't climb about on it, because we said we wouldn't. But I'd like to see it.'

'I'd like to go right into the castle,' said Jack.

'No, no!' said Tassie, her eyes widening as if she was

scared. The others looked at her with interest.

'Why not?' asked Jack. 'It's empty, isn't it?'

'No, it's not empty,' said Tassie. 'There are voices and cryings and the sound of feet. It is not a good place to go.'

'You've been listening to gossip,' said Philip. 'Who would be there now? There's no coming and going, there's no one ever seen about the castle! It's only the owls hooting there, or the bats squeaking or something.'

'What's the old story about the castle?' asked Dinah. 'Do you know it, Tassie?'

'It's said that a wicked man lived there once, who got people to visit him in his castle – and they were never heard of again,' said Tassie, speaking in a low voice as if she was afraid that the wicked man, whoever he was, might hear her. 'They heard cries and groans, and the clashing of swords. It is said, too, that he used to lock people up in hidden rooms, and starve them to death.'

'What a nice old man!' said Philip, with a laugh. 'I don't believe a word of it. You always get these stories about old places. I expect some half-mad old fellow came along, bought the old castle, patched it up, and lived there pretending to be an old-time baron or something. He must have been mad to live in a lonely place like that.'

'He had plenty of horses, they say, and they used this road every day,' said Tassie. 'Did you notice how here and there, in the steepest places, the road was cobbled? That was to help the horses.'

'Yes, I did notice a cobbled bit just now,' said Philip. The others were silent for a minute. Somehow the fact that the road really was cobbled here and there made them think there might be something in the story Tassie had told them.

'Anyway, that all happened years ago, and the old man's gone, and nobody's there,' said Philip. 'I'd love to explore all over the castle. Wouldn't you, Jack?'

'Rather!' said Jack. And Kiki agreed, swaying to and fro

on his shoulder. 'Rather,' said Kiki, 'rather, rather, rather, ra . . .'

'Kiki get off my shoulder for a bit,' panted Jack. 'You feel jolly heavy up this hill.'

'Kiki I'll have you!' said Tassie, and Kiki flew to her at once, informing her that she had better open her book at page six. Tassie did not pant and puff as the others did. She was like a goat, the way she sprang up the steepest places and never seemed in the least tired.

'Hallo – we're a good way up at last!' said Philip, wiping his hot forehead. 'Look, the road goes all strange here.'

So it did. It could no longer be called a road, for part of the hillside had fallen away and had piled itself on the road and all around. Enormous boulders of rock lay where they had rolled, and the stumps of trees showed where the moving hillside had cut them into pieces.

The children gazed over the untidy, rock-strewn landscape. 'It looks as if an earthquake had upset it,' said Lucy-Ann.

Beyond the landslide stood the castle, looking even more enormous now. The children could see how strongly built it was, and could see two of the square towers, with the long battlemented wall stretching between them.

'I'd like to go up into one of those towers,' said Philip longingly. 'What a marvellous view we'd get!'

'The castle isn't really right on top of the hill,' said Jack, 'though it looks as if it is from down below. Doesn't it look fierce, somehow!'

It did. None of the children thought it was a very nice castle. It seemed to be such a lonely, strange, sinister place. It frowned over the hillside, and was not at all welcoming. All the same, it was exciting.

'Tassie, how do we get to the back of it?' asked Philip, turning to the little girl. 'We *could* climb over this landslide bit, I suppose, but we said we wouldn't, and anyhow some of those boulders look as if they would like to go rolling over and over down the hillside if anybody gave them a little push!'

'There's my eagle again!' cried Jack suddenly, in excitement, and he pointed to a big bird that rose soaring in the air, above the castle. 'See it? It *is* an eagle, no doubt about it. Isn't it enormous? I bet it's got a nest somewhere about. Oh golly, there's another of them, look!'

Sure enough there were two magnificent eagles rising in the air. They rose higher and higher, and the children watched them, fascinated.

'How do they soar upwards like that without moving their wings?' asked Lucy-Ann. 'I could understand it if they soared downwards – glide, you know – but to go up and up and up – gracious, they're only just specks.'

'They use air-currents I expect,' said Jack. 'Must be plenty on a hill-top. *Two* eagles – and together. Well, that settles it – there must be a nest!'

'You're not thinking of taming a young eagle, I hope?' said Dinah, in alarm.

'Don't worry. Kiki would never let Jack have a tame eagle,' said Lucy-Ann.

This was true, and Dinah heaved a sigh of relief.

'They rose from somewhere behind the castle as far as I could see,' said Jack eagerly. 'Let's go round and see if we can find out where their nest is. Come on.'

They left the strange, untidy landslide, and, following Tassie, made their way to the east, climbing over the hillside with difficulty. Tassie led them to a winding little path, narrow but safe.

'Whose path is this?' said Dinah in surprise.

'The rabbits' path,' said Tassie. 'There are millions here. They make quite good little paths all over the place.'

'I can't go any further!' panted Lucy-Ann after some

while. 'I'm tired out. Let's rest and have our tea. The eagles' nest won't run away.'

Everyone thought that was a good idea. They flopped down on the grass, panting. Philip slung his knapsack round to his chest and undid it. He handed out the food, and then lay flat on the ground. Button immediately began to lick his face all over.

It was lovely to have a drink, though there wasn't nearly enough. No-one seemed very hungry, but Button and Kiki managed quite a few sandwiches between them. Tassie had a few too. She was the least tired out of any of them. She sat and scratched Kiki's head, whilst the others lay flat on the hillside.

They soon recovered and sat up. Philip heard the trickling of water somewhere near by and went to investigate. He still felt terribly thirsty. He called back to the others:

'The spring that runs past our cottage runs here. It's lovely and cold. Anyone want a drink?'

Everybody did. They got up and went to the little spring that gushed out from a hole in the hillside and then ran and leapt over the pebbly bed until it once more disappeared into the earth, to come out again further down.

The children bathed their hot feet in the cool water. Then Jack caught sight of his precious eagles again. 'Come on! We'll see where they fly down to. I wish I'd brought my camera! I could have photographed their nest!'

6

How can they get in?

They were near to the castle by now. The great, thick walls rose up, far above their heads. There was no break in them, except about sixteen feet up, where slit windows could be seen.

'It's built of the big boulders we see all over the hillside,' said Philip. 'It must have been very hard work to take so many up here to build the castle. Look – over there are some bigger windows. I suppose that wicked old fellow Tassie was telling us about liked to have a little more light in his castle than slit windows give. It's a funny place. You can quite well see where it has been patched up can't you?'

'There are the eagles again!' cried Jack. 'They're gliding down – and down. Watch them everyone!'

The little company stood and watched the two big birds, whose span of wings was really enormous.

'They've gone down inside the castle courtyard,' said Jack. 'That's where they've got their nest, I bet! In the courtyard somewhere. I simply must find it.'

'But you can't possibly get into the courtyard,' said Philip.

'Where's the gateway of the castle?' demanded Jack, turning to Tassie.

'At the front, where that landslide is,' said Tassie. 'You couldn't get over the landslide without being in danger, and anyway if you did, you'd find the great gate shut. There's another door, further along here, but that's locked. You can't get into the castle.'

'Where's the door along here?' said Jack. They went further along, turned a corner of the castle wall, and came to a sturdy oak door, flush with the wall. The wall arched over it, and the door fitted exactly. Jack put his eye to the keyhole but could see nothing.

'Do you mean to tell me there's no other way into this castle?' he said to Tassie. 'What a peculiar place! It's like a prison.'

'That's what it was,' said Lucy-Ann, shivering as she remembered the story Tassie had told. 'A prison for poor wretched people who came here and couldn't get away – and were never heard of again!'

Jack was in despair. To think that two rare eagles might be nesting in the courtyard on the other side of the wall – and he couldn't get at them. It was too bad.

'We must get in, we simply must,' he said, and gazed up at the high windows. But there was no way of getting up there. The walls were far too smooth to climb. There was no ivy. The castle was impregnable.

'People would have got in before now if there had been a way,' said Philip. 'It just shows there's no way in if no one ever comes here.'

'Tassie – don't *you* know of a way?' said Jack, turning to the little girl. She considered solemnly. Then she nodded her head.

'I might know,' she said. 'I have never been. But it might be a way.'

'Show us, quickly!' said Jack eagerly.

Tassie led them further round the castle, towards the back of it. Here it was built almost into the cliff. A narrow, dark pathway led between the steep hillside and the back wall of the castle. It was almost a tunnel, for both wall and cliff practically met at one place.

Tassie came to a stop, and pointed up. The other four looked, and saw that there was one of the slit windows high up above them. They stared at Tassie, not seeing in the least how that helped them.

'Don't you see?' said Tassie. 'You could climb up the

cliffside here, because it is all overgrown with creepers – and then, when you get opposite that window, you might put a branch of a tree across or something, and get in.'

'I see what she means!' said Philip. 'If we could lug a plank or a bough up the side of the steep cliff here, that the castle backs on to – and put one end of it on to the windowsill, and the other firmly into the cliff – we could slide across and get in! It's an idea!'

The rest of the company received this news with mixed feelings. Dinah was already afraid of bats in the dark and narrow passageway, and would willingly have gone back into the sunshine of the open hillside. Lucy-Ann didn't like the idea of climbing the cliff and sliding across a dangerous branch that might slip, into the silent and deserted castle. Jack, on the other hand, thought it was well worth trying, and was eager to do so at once.

'Put on the light,' said Kiki earnestly from somewhere in the dark passage. 'Put on the light.'

The children laughed. It was funny the way Kiki sometimes said what sounded like a very sensible sentence.

'Let's find a branch or something,' said Jack. So they went out of the musty-smelling passage, and hunted for something to use as a bridge across to the window of the castle.

But there was nothing to be found at all. True, Philip found a dead branch, but it was so dead that it would have cracked at once under anyone's weight. It was impossible to break off from a tree a branch big enough to be any use.

'Blow!' said Jack. 'Anyway, let's go back and see if we can climb up opposite the window. If we think we *could* get in the way Tassie suggests, we might come up tomorrow with a plank.'

'Yes, it would be better to leave it till tomorrow, really,' said Dinah, trying to see the time by her watch. 'It's getting rather late now. Let's come up tomorrow with your camera, Jack.'

'All right. But we'll just see if it's possible to climb in at that window first,' said Jack. He tried to climb up the cliffside, but it was very steep, and he kept slipping down. Then Philip tried, and, by means of holding on tightly to some of the strongest of the creepers, he pulled himself up a little way.

But the creeper broke, and down he came, missing his footing at the bottom, and rolling over and over. Fortunately, except for a few bruises, he wasn't hurt.

'I'll go,' said Tassie. And up she went like a monkey. It was extraordinary the way she could climb. She was far better than any of them. She seemed to know just where to put her feet, and just which creeper to hold on to.

Soon she was opposite the slit window. The creepers grew very thickly on the cliff-side there, and she held on to them whilst she peered across at the window.

'I believe I could almost jump across to the sill,' she called to the others.

'Don't you do anything of the sort,' shouted back Philip at once. 'Little donkey! You'd break both your legs if you fell! What can you see?'

'Nothing much!' called back Tassie, who still seemed to be considering whether or not to jump across and chance it. 'There's the window – very narrow, or course. I don't know if we could squeeze through. And past the window I can see a room, but it's so dark I can't see if it's big or small or anything. It looks very strange.'

'I bet it does!' said Jack. 'Come on down, Tassie.'

'I'll just leap across and have a try at squeezing in,' said Tassie, and poised herself for a jump. But a roar from Philip stopped her.

'If you do that we'll never let you go with us again. Do you hear? You'll break your legs!'

Tassie thought better of her idea. The threat of never being allowed to go about with the children she so much liked and admired filled her with horror. She contented herself with one more look across at the window, and then she climbed down like a goat, landing directly beside the waiting children.

'It's just as well that you did as you were told,' said Philip grimly. 'Suppose you had got across – and squeezed inside – and then couldn't get out again! You'd have been a prisoner in that castle for ever and ever!'

Tassie said nothing. She had great faith in her powers of climbing and jumping, and she thought Philip was making a fuss about nothing. Kiki, hearing Philip's stern voice, joined in the scolding.

'How many times have I told you to shut the door?' she said, flying on to Tassie's shoulder. Tassie laughed and scratched Kiki's poll.

'Only about a hundred times,' she said, and the others laughed too. They made their way out of the dark tunnel-like passage, and were glad to be in the sun again.

'Well, we know what to do, anyway,' said Jack. 'We'll find a plank or something to bring up here tomorrow, and we'll send Tassie up with it, and she can put it across from the cliffside to the window. We'll give her a strong rope too, so that she can knot it to some of that creeper up there, and we can pull on it to help ourselves up. We're not as goat-footed as Tassie.'

'No, she's marvellous,' said Lucy-Ann, and Tassie glowed with pleasure. They made their way down the hillside again, finding it a little easier to climb down than up, especially as Tassie took them a good way she knew.

'It's really getting very late,' said Jack. 'I hope your mother won't be anxious, Philip.'

'Oh no,' said Philip. 'She'd know one of us would run down for help if anything happened.'

All the same, Mrs Mannering *had* been wondering what had become of the children and she was very glad to see them. She had supper ready for them, and Tassie was asked to stay too. She was thrilled, and tried to watch how the others ate and drank, as she had never been invited out before. Kiki sat on Jack's shoulder, and fed on titbits that Jack and the others handed her, making odd remarks from time to time about putting the kettle on, and using handkerchiefs. Button curled up on Philip's knee and went sound asleep. He was tired after his long walk, though Philip had carried him a good way.

'You know, I half thought Button might run off when we took him out on the hillside he knows so well,' said Philip. 'But he didn't. He didn't even seem to think of it.'

'He's a darling,' said Lucy-Ann, looking at the sleeping fox club, who had curled his sharp little nose into his big tail. 'It's a pity he's a bit smelly.'

'Well, he'll get worse,' said Philip. 'So you might as well get used to it. Foxes do smell. I expect we smell just as strong to them.'

'Oh! I'm sure we don't,' thought Lucy-Ann. 'Oh dear, how sleepy I am!'

They were all sleepy that night. The long climb in the sunshine had tired them out. 'Let's go to bed,' said Philip with such a loud yawn that Button woke up with a jump. 'We've got an exciting day tomorrow, with a lot of climbing again. Don't forget to look out your camera, Jack.'

'Oh yes – I simply *must* take a snap of the eagles!' said Jack. 'Golly, we'll have some fun tomorrow!'

Then up they went to bed, yawning. Kiki yawned the loudest – not that she was tired, but it was a lovely noise to copy!

7

Inside the castle of adventure

The next day Button woke Philip by licking the bare sole of his foot, which was sticking out from the bedclothes. Philip woke with a yell, for he was very ticklish there.

'Stop it, Jack!' he shouted, and then looked in surprise across the room, where Jack was just opening startled eyes. 'Oh – it's all right – it's only Button. Button, you are never to lick the soles of my feet!'

Jack sat up, grinning. He rubbed his eyes and stretched. Then his glance fell on his fine camera, which he had put ready to take up the hill with him that day, and he remembered what they had planned.

'Come on – let's get up,' he said to Philip, and jumped out of bed. 'It's a gorgeous day, and I'm longing to go up to the castle again. I might get some wonderful pictures of those eagles.'

Philip was almost as interested in birds as Jack was. The boys began to talk about eagles as they dressed. They banged at the girls' door as they went down. Mrs Mannering was already up, for she was an early riser. A smell of frying bacon arose on the air.

'Lovely!' said Jack sniffing. 'Kiki, don't stick your claws so hard into my shoulder. I got sunburnt yesterday and it hurts.'

'What a pity, what a pity!' said Kiki, in sorrowful tones. The boys laughed.

'You'd almost think she really did understand what you say,' said Philip.

'She does!' said Jack. 'I say, what about getting a plank or something now, whilst we're waiting for breakfast – you know, to put across to the windowsill of the castle?'

'Right,' said Philip, and they wandered out into the sunshine, still sniffing the delicious smell of frying bacon, to which was now added the fragrance of coffee. Button trotted at Philip's heels, nibbling them gently every time the boy stopped. He did not dare to go near Jack, for if he did Kiki swooped down on him in a fury, and snapped her curved beak at him.

The boys went into the shed where the car was kept. They soon found just what they wanted – a stout plank long enough to reach from the cliff wall to the sill. 'Golly! It will be pretty heavy to carry!' said Jack. 'We'll all have to take turns at it. It wouldn't do to have a smaller one – it just might not reach.'

The girls came out and the boys showed them what they had found. In the night Lucy-Ann had made up her mind she wouldn't do any plank-climbing or castle-exploring, but now, in the warm golden sunshine, she altered her mind, and felt that she couldn't possibly be left out of even a small adventure.

'Mother, could we go off for the whole day this time?' said Philip. 'Jack's got his camera ready. We're pretty certain we know where those eagles are now, and we shall perhaps be able to take some good pictures of them.'

'Well, it's a lovely day, so it would do you good to go off picnicking,' said his mother. 'Oh, do stop Kiki taking the marmalade, Jack! Really, I shan't have that bird at the table any more, if you can't make it behave. It ate half the raspberry jam at tea yesterday.'

'Take your nose out of the marmalade, Kiki,' said Jack sternly, and Kiki sat back on his shoulder, offended. She began to imitate Mrs Mannering crunching up toast, eyeing her balefully the whole time, annoyed at being robbed of the marmalade. Mrs Mannering had to laugh.

'You're not going on that landslide, are you?' she said,

and the children shook their heads.

'No, Mother. Tassie showed us another way. Hallo, here she is. Tassie, have you had your breakfast?'

Tassie was peeping in at the kitchen window, her eyes bright under their tangle of hair. Mrs Mannering sighed. 'I might as well not have bothered myself to give her a bath,' she said. 'She's just as dirty as ever. I did think that she would like feeling clean.'

'She doesn't,' said Dinah. 'All she liked was that smell of carbolic, Mother. If you want to make Tassie wash herself, you'll have to present her with a bar of strong carbolic soap!'

Tassie, it appeared, had had her breakfast some time before. She climbed in at the window and accepted a piece of toast and marmalade from Philip. Kiki at once edged over to her hopefully. She liked toast and marmalade. Tassie shared it with the parrot.

The five children set off soon after breakfast. Dinah carried the knapsack of food. Lucy-Ann carried Jack's precious camera. Tassie carried Kiki on her shoulder, very proudly indeed. The two boys carried the plank between them.

'Take us the shortest way you know, Tassie,' begged Jack. 'This plank is so awkward to carry. I say, Philip, did you think to bring a rope too? I forgot.'

'I've tied one round my waist,' said Philip. 'It's long enough, I think. Button, don't get under my feet like that, and don't ask to be carried when I've got to take this tiresome plank up the hill!'

With many rests, the little party went up the steep hill towards the castle. Jack kept a lookout for the eagles, but he didn't see either of them. Kiki flew off to have a few words with some rooks they met, and then flew back again to Tassie's shoulder. She couldn't understand why Tassie carried shoes round her neck, and pecked curiously at the laces, trying to get them out of the shoes.

At last they arrived at the castle, and made their way round the great wall to the back, where the wall of the castle ran level with the side of the hill.

'Here we are at last,' said Jack, panting, and put the plank down thankfully. 'You girls coming into the passageway to watch us putting the plank in place, or not?'

'Yes, rather,' said Dinah. They all went into the tunnel-like passage, which smelt mustier than ever, after the clean heathery smell outside.

They came to where they had climbed up the day before. 'Tassie, you go up first, and tie this rope firmly to a stout creeper stem,' said Philip, giving her the rope, which he had untied from his waist. 'Then we can all pull ourselves up by it without slipping.'

Tassie climbed up the creeper-clad wall easily. She stopped opposite the slit window of the castle. She tied the rope firmly round a strong creeper stem, and then tested it by leaning forward with all her weight on it.

'Look out, silly!' shouted Philip. 'If that rope gives you'll fall on top of us.'

But it didn't give. It was quite safe. Tassie grinned down at them and then slid down, holding the rope, and landed beside them on her toes.

'You ought to be in a circus,' said Jack. But Tassie looked blank. She had no idea what a circus was.

Philip had another, shorter piece of rope. 'That's to haul up the plank with,' he said. 'Now, let's tie the plank firmly with this rope, and I'll drag it up after me as I climb up. Here goes!'

Holding with one hand on to the rope that now hung down from the creeper, and with the other to the rope that dragged the plank, Philip started up the steep cliff wall. But he needed both hands to help himself up, and had to slide down again.

'Tie the plank to my waist,' he said to Jack. 'Then I can have both hands to help myself up with, and the plank will come up behind me by itself.'

So the plank was tied to his waist, and then the boy went up again, this time pulling himself with both hands on the rope. His feet slipped, but he went on upwards, feeling the drag of the heavy plank on his waist.

At last he was opposite the castle window. He could see nothing inside the window at all, except black darkness. He began to try and clear a place to fix in one edge of the plank.

'Look out – I'm coming up too to help,' called Jack from below, and up he came, pulling on Tassie's rope. Then, between them, they managed to haul up the plank, and lift it so that it almost reached the windowsill.

'A bit more over – that's right – now a bit more to the right!' panted Jack – and then, with a thud, the plank at last rested on the sill of the narrow slit window. The other end rested firmly on a mass of tangled creeper roots, and on some stout ivy stems.

Jack tested the plank. It seemed quite firm. Philip tested it too. Yes, it seemed safe enough.

'Have you really fixed it?' shouted Dinah, in excitement. 'Jolly good! Look out, there goes Kiki!'

Sure enough, Kiki, who had been watching everything in the greatest surprise, had sailed up in the air and was now sitting on the plank, raising her crest and making a chortling noise. Then she walked clumsily across to the window and hopped on the sill. She poked her beak inside the opening. There was no glass there, of course.

'Kiki always likes to poke her nose into everything!' said Lucy-Ann. 'Can we come up now, Philip?'

'We're just making a flat place among all these roots and things, so that you can stand here safely till we can help you across,' said Philip, stamping on the creepers around. 'The cliff wall goes in a bit just here – you can almost sit down, if I mess the creepers about a bit.'

'I'll go across the plank,' said Jack. But a shout from Lucy-Ann stopped him.

'No, Jack. Wait till I'm up there. I want to see you properly! I can only see your legs from down here.'

Soon all three girls were up by the boys. It was easy to go up by the rope. They watched Jack sit astride the plank, and gradually edge himself across in that position. The plank was as firm as could be. Jack felt quite safe.

He got to the windowsill. He stood up on the plank and clutched the stone sides of the narrow window. He stood in the opening.

'Golly, it's narrow!' he shouted across the plank, to where the others were watching him breathlessly. 'I don't believe I can squeeze through!'

'Well, if you can't *I* certainly shan't be able to,' said Philip. 'Go on – try. You're not as fat as all that, surely!'

Jack began to squeeze through the narrow stone window. It certainly was a squash. He had to hold his tummy in hard, and not breathe at all. He wriggled through gradually, and then suddenly jumped to the floor the other side. He yelled back.

'Hurrah, I'm through! Come on, everyone. I'm in a pitch-black room. We'll have to bring torches next time.'

Dinah went next, helped by Philip. Jack helped her down the other side. She hadn't much difficulty in getting through the window. Then came Tassie, then Lucy-Ann, then Philip, who had as much difficulty as Jack in squeezing through.

'Well, here we are!' he said, 'inside the Castle of Adventure!'

8

Up in the tower

'The Castle of Adventure!' echoed Lucy-Ann in surprise. 'What makes you say that? Do you think we shall have an adventure here?'

'Oh, I don't know!' said Philip. 'I just said it – but it's got an odd feeling, this castle, hasn't it? My word, isn't it dark?'

A mournful barking came from below. It was Button, left behind. Philip stuck his head out of the window. 'It's all right, Button. We're coming back!'

Kiki stuck her head out too, and gave a railway engine screech. 'That's just to tell poor Button she's up here, and he's not!' said Dinah. 'Kiki, you do like to crow over poor Button, don't you?'

It was very dark in the room they had jumped into. But gradually they could see better as their eyes got used to the darkness. The children blinked and tried to see their surroundings.

'It's just a big bare room,' said Jack, rather disappointed. He didn't quite know what he had expected to see. 'I suppose the whole castle's like this – full of big, bare, cold rooms. Come on – let's do a bit of exploring.'

They made their way to the door, which opened into a long corridor. They went down this and came to a lighter room, lit by one slit window and one wide one evidently added much later. This room had a big fireplace and there were still old grey ashes there. The children looked at them.

'Funny to think that people once sat round that fire!' said Dinah. They went into the next room, which again was very dark, because it had only a slit window to light it. Dinah wandered to the window, and suddenly gave such a yell that everyone jumped violently.

'Dinah! What is it?' cried Philip.

Dinah ran back to him so quickly that she bumped into him. 'There's something in this room!' she cried. 'It touched my hair. I felt it. Come out quickly.'

'Don't be silly,' began Philip, and then he stopped suddenly. Something had touched his hair too! He swung round but there was nothing there. His heart beat fast. Was there really something in the room, touching them, but invisible?

Then a ray of sunlight unexpectedly came slanting in through the slit window, and Philip gave a sudden laugh. 'How silly we are!' he said. 'It's cobwebs – look, hanging down from the ceiling! They must be years old!'

Everyone was very much relieved, but Dinah wouldn't stay in the room one moment more. She was scared – and the very idea of cobwebs touching her made her more scared still. She shuddered when she thought of the spiders that might drop on her from the cobwebby ceiling!

'Come out where it's sunshiny,' she begged, and they all went into a wide corridor, where the sun poured in at many windows. Tassie walked close to Philip, with scared eyes. She knew the old village tales, and half expected the wicked old man to appear from somewhere and take them all prisoner! But where Philip went she meant to go too.

'Look – this way leads across one of the battlemented walls to the eastern tower!' cried Jack. 'Let's go along to the tower – we'll get a magnificent view from there.'

'I feel like an old-time soldier marching round the castle wall,' said Philip, as they made their way along to the tower. 'Here we are. Goodness, it's quite big, isn't it? Look, there's a room at the bottom of the tower, flush with this wall – and there's a winding stone stair that leads to the top of the tower. Come on, up we go!'

And up they went, determined not to look at the view till they got to the highest point. The stone stair twisted awkwardly round and round, and led them straight into another room, out of which a narrow stair led them to the very roof of the tower itself.

They went up the tiny stair and found themselves on the top of the tower, its battlemented edge rising a few feet all round.

They all gasped, and gazed down in silence. Not one of them had ever been so high up before, nor had they seen such a wide and magnificent view. It seemed as if the whole world lay spread out before them, sparkling in the sunshine. Below, far, far below, lay the valley, through which curved the silver river, like a gleaming snake. What houses they could see looked like toy ones.

'Look at those hills opposite,' said Jack. 'There are hills behind those – and hills behind those too – and hills behind those!'

Tassie was amazed. She never thought the world was so big. From the vantage point of the high tower the whole country was spread like a living map before her. It was so beautiful that for some extraordinary reason Lucy-Ann felt like crying.

'What a wonderful place this must have been for a lookout!' said Philip. 'Any sentry here could see enemies coming miles and miles away. Look – is that Spring Cottage right down there, among those trees?'

It was, looking like a doll's house, halfway down the hill. 'I wish we could bring Mother up here,' said Dinah. 'How she would love this view!'

'Look! Look! There are the eagles again!' said Jack, and he pointed up in the air, where two great eagles soared to the clouds. 'I say – shall we have our lunch here, on the top of this tower, and see this marvellous view all the time, and watch my eagles?'

'Oh *yes!*' said everyone, including Kiki. She always joined in any chorus.

'Poor little Button,' said Philip. 'I wish we could have brought him too. But it was too risky across that plank. I expect he's feeling very lonely now. I hope he won't run off.'

'You know he won't,' said Dinah. 'No animal ever runs away from you, worse luck. Oh, *Philip* – you haven't brought that awful toad with you, have you? Yes, you have! It's peeping out of your neck! I just won't sit up here with a toad crawling round.'

'Now for goodness' sake don't start a quarrel up on the top of the tower,' said Jack, in real alarm. 'That stone edging won't stop anyone from falling if they start fooling about. Dinah, do sit down.'

'Don't order me about,' said Dinah, beginning to flare up.

'Where's the food?' said Lucy-Ann, hoping to change the subject. 'Dinah, you've got it. Get it out, because I'm dying of hunger!'

Keeping as far away from her brother as she could, Dinah undid the knapsack. There were two big packets inside, one marked 'Dinner' and one marked 'Tea.'

'Put the tea packet back,' said Jack, 'or we might gobble that up too! I feel hungry enough to eat all you've got there.'

Dinah divided out sandwiches, cake, biscuits, fruit and chocolate. Then she presented everyone with a cardboard cup of lemonade from a bottle.

'We've had plenty of picnics in our time,' said Philip, biting hugely into a thick sandwich of egg and ham, 'but never one in such an extraordinary place as this. It almost makes me giddy, looking out at that enormous view.'

'It's lovely to sit here and eat, looking at those hills, and that winding river down in the valley,' said Lucy-An contentedly. 'I believe that old man Tassie told us about must have bought this castle for the view! I would, I know, if I had enough money.'

They ate and drank happily. Kiki shared the sandwiches, which she liked immensely. Then she went exploring along the stone coping at the edge of the tower, climbing upside-down now and again.

The children watched her, eating their cake. Suddenly Kiki gave an alarming screech, lost her balance and fell right off the tower! She disappeared below, and the children leapt up in horror. Then they sat down again, smiling and feeling rather foolish – for, of course, as soon as she fell, Kiki spread out her wings and soared into the air!

'Idiot, Kiki!' said Dinah. 'You gave me quite a scare! Well, has everyone nearly finished? If so, I'll clear up the paper and the cardboard cups and put them back into the knapsack.'

Jack had been watching the eagles, which, all the time they were at lunch, had been soaring high in the air, looking like black specks. Now they were coming down again, gliding in large circles, their great wings spread out to catch the smallest current of air.

There was plenty of wind on the top of the hill. It blew steadily on the tower, and the children's hair was blown back all the time, as they sat facing the breeze. They watched the eagles go lower and lower.

Below them and behind them lay the inner courtyard of the castle. It was overgrown with grass and patches of heather. Gorse bushes grew there, and a few small birch-trees. The hillside had come into its own again there, and pushed up by strong-growing bushes, which had forced their way between them.

'I believe the eagles have their nest in that clump of trees over there, in the corner of the overgrown courtyard!' said Jack excitedly. 'It's the sort of craggy place they might choose! Shall we go and see?'

'Are you sure they're not dangerous?' said Philip doubtfully. 'They're awfully big birds – and I *have* heard stories of them attacking men.'

'Yes,' said Jack. 'Well – as soon as they fly off again, I'll go and look. Anyway, we might as well go down now and have a look round. Kiki, come here!'

Kiki flew to his shoulder, and nibbled his ear gently, talking her usual nonsense. The children got up and went down the two stone stairways. Both the top and bottom rooms of the tower were completely empty. Cobwebs hung in the corners, and dust lay thickly on the floor and ledges, except where the wind blew in strongly.

'How do we get down to the courtyard?' wondered Philip. 'We'll have to go back along the wall and into the castle itself, I suppose. There must be a stairway down to the rooms below.'

So back they went, and came to the main building of the castle again. They looked into room after room, all empty. Then at last they came to a very wide stone stairway that led down and down. They clattered down it and came into a big hall. It was dark.

Something suddenly hurled itself against Philip's legs and he leapt in fright, giving a loud exclamation. Everyone stood still.

'What is it?' said Lucy-Ann, in a whisper.

It was Button, the fox cub! 'Now how in the world did *he* get to us!' cried Philip, picking the little creature up. 'He must have found some hole, I suppose, and scrambled through it to find us. Button, you're a marvel! But my word, you did give me a fright!'

Button gave some of his little barks as he cuddled against Philip's chest. Kiki addressed a few scornful remarks to him about shutting the door. She was the only one sorry to see his arrival!

'Now let's get into the courtyard and explore round a bit,' said Jack. 'Look out for the eagles, all of you!'

9

The eagle's nest

The children picked their way over the big, overgrown courtyard. It was an absolute wilderness now, though with a little imagination they could picture what it must have been like in the old days – a vast stone-paved place, hewn out of the hillside itself, with craggy pieces towering up at the far ends.

'It's in one of those craggy places that I think the eagles have got their nest,' said Jack, as they picked their way across the hot courtyard. 'Tassie, take Kiki for me, will you, and hang on to her. I don't want her interfering just now.'

Tassie proudly took Kiki, and stood still whilst the others went towards a towering piece of rock, clothed here and there with heather, that rose up at one end of the courtyard. Lucy-Ann didn't particularly want to go too near to the eagles, but she wanted to be with Jack.

'You girls stay down at the bottom of this crag,' said Jack. 'I'm going to climb up with Philip. I don't think the eagles will attack us, Philip, in fact I'm pretty sure they won't; but look out, in case.'

The boys were just beginning to climb when a loud, yelping scream made them stop and clutch at one another in fright. The girls jumped violently. Button ran into the nearest rabbit-hole and stayed there. Only Kiki did not seem to be frightened.

Into Tassie's mind jumped the thought that the scream must be from one of the wicked man's poor prisoners! Perhaps he wasn't dead, perhaps he was still there somewhere. The other children were not so foolish as to think things like this, but the scream certainly made their blood run cold!

'What was it, Jack?' whispered Lucy-Ann. 'Come back. Don't go up there. The scream came from there.'

It came again, more loudly – a curious, almost yelping noise. Kiki cleared her throat to imitate it. What a fine noise to copy!

She gave a remarkably good imitation of the scream and made everyone jump again. Tassie almost fell over, for Kiki was on her shoulder.

'Bad bird! Naughty bird!' said Jack fiercely, in a low voice. Kiki looked at him. From her throat came the scream again – and almost at the same moment a great eagle, which must have been somewhere on the rocky crag, rose up in the air on enormous wings, and soared over the little company, looking down in amazement to see who had made such a noise.

And then, from the eagle's own throat, there came again the yelping scream the children had heard!

'Gosh – it was the eagle screaming, that's all!' said Jack, in relief. 'Why didn't I think of that? I've never heard one before. That shows their nest must be somewhere up here. Come on, Philip.'

The eagle did not swoop down to the children, but glided above them, looking down. Its interest was centred on Kiki, who feeling rather thrilled at having found such a good new noise, yelped again.

The eagle answered and flew lower. Kiki went up to meet it, looking very small compared with the big eagle. The children could plainly see the long yellowish feathers on the nape of its neck, shining in the sunlight.

'It *is* a golden eagle,' said Lucy-Ann. 'Jack was right. Look at those golden feathers! Oh dear – I hope it doesn't come any lower.'

All the five children watched Kiki and the eagle. Usually birds were either puzzled and afraid of Kiki, or angry. But the eagle was neither. It seemed intensely interested, as if wondering how it was that this queer looking little bird, so unlike an eagle, could make eagle noises!

Kiki was enjoying herself. She flew about the eagle, yelping to it, and then suddenly changed her mind and told it to blow its nose.

At the sound of an apparently human voice the eagle sheered off a little, still gazing in interest at Kiki. Finally, taking no notice at all of the children, it flew upwards to a high rock on the crag, and perched there, looking down in a very royal fashion.

'Isn't it a magnificent bird?' said Jack in the utmost delight. 'Fancy us seeing an eagle at close quarters like this! Look at its frowning brows, and its piercing eyes! I don't wonder it's called the king of the birds!'

The eagle was a truly splendid sight, as it sat there like a king. It was feathered in dark brown, except for the golden streaks on the nape of its neck. Its legs were covered in feathers almost to the claws. It watched Kiki unblinkingly.

'There's the second eagle, look!' said Lucy-Ann suddenly, in a low voice. The children saw the other eagle rising up into the air from the crag, evidently curious to see what was happening. It soared upwards, spreading out its strong pinions like fingers, the wing-tips curving up as it went. Then, quite suddenly, the first eagle tired of Kiki, flapped its enormous wings, and joined its mate.

'The first eagle is the male, the second one is the female,' said Jack excitedly.

'How do you know?' asked Dinah disbelievingly. She couldn't see any difference at all.

'The second one is bigger than the first,' said Jack. 'The female golden eagle is always the bigger of the two; bigger wing-span too. Golly, I do feel thrilled.'

'You ought to have snapped that eagle sitting on the crag,' said Philip. Jack gave an exclamation of annoyance.

'Blow! I never even thought of my camera! I was so absorbed in watching the birds. What marvellous pictures I could take!'

The two birds were now only specks in the sky, for they had soared up to an immense height. 'It would be a jolly good chance to explore this crag for their nest whilst they are safely up there,' said Jack. 'It's funny they don't seem scared of us, isn't it? I suppose they know hardly anything of man, always living up here on this hilltop.'

'I can't imagine what's happened to Button,' said Philip anxiously. 'He went down that hole and he's not back yet.'

'Probably scaring a family of rabbits out of their senses!' said Jack. 'He'll come back all right. I'm not surprised he went down a rabbit hole when he heard that scream. I'd have gone down one myself if I could! It was an awful noise.'

The boys began to climb up again. It was fairly stiff going for the little crag was steep and rocky. Its top was almost as high as the nearby tower.

On the western side, well hidden in a little hollow, Jack found what he wanted – the eagles' nest!

'Look!' he said, 'look! Did you ever see such an enormous thing, Philip! It must be six feet wide at the bottom!'

The boys looked at the great nest on the broad ledge of rock. It was about two feet high, made of twigs and small boughs, with heather tucked in between. The cup of the nest was almost a foot and a half across, and very well lined with moss, grass and bits of heather.

'There's a young one in the nest!' said Jack, in delight. 'Quite a big bird too – must be more than three months old, and ready to fly.'

The young bird crouched down in the nest when it heard Jack's voice. It was already so big that Philip would hardly have known it was a nestling. But Jack's sure eye had noticed the white bases of the feathers, telling him that this was a young eagle, and not an old one.

Kiki flew inquisitively to the nest. She gave a yelp like the eagle had made. The young bird looked up enquringly, recognized the sound but not the maker of it.

'Your camera, quick!' whispered Philip, and Jack began to adjust his camera with quick, eager fingers.

'Quick, the old eagles are coming back,' whispered Philip, and Jack gave a glance upwards. The eagles had remembered their young one, and seeing the boys so near the nest were coming down to see what was happening.

Jack snapped the camera just in time, for Kiki flew off almost immediately to meet the eagles, screaming a welcome.

'Better get down now,' said Philip, thinking that the two old eagles looked pretty fierce. 'My word, I wish we could take pictures of that young one learning to fly. It looks as if it will take off from the nest any day now.'

With the two eagles gliding not far above them the boys climbed down as hastily as they could. 'Did you get a snap?' asked Lucy-Ann eagerly, and Jack nodded. He looked excited.

'I shall have to come back again,' he said. 'Do you know, I might get finer close-up pictures of eagles than anyone has ever got before? Think of that! I'd make a lot of money out of them, I daresay, and I'd have them in all kind of nature magazines.'

'Oh, Jack – do take some more pictures then,' said Lucy-Ann, her eyes shining.

'I'd have to almost *live* up here, to take good ones,' said Jack. 'It's no good just coming up on the off-chance. If only I could spend a few days here!'

'Well – I suppose you could, if you wanted to,' said Philip. 'I expect Mother would let you, if you told her about the eagles. It would be quite safe up here, and we could bring you food.'

'Can't we *all* come and stay up here for a few days?' said Lucy-Ann, who didn't want her brother to be away from them. 'Why can't we?'

'Well – you know we can't leave my mother all alone down there,' said Philip. 'She'd think it was jolly mean.'

'Oh yes – of course,' said Lucy-Ann, going rather red. 'I never thought of that. How awful of me!'

'All the same, I don't see why *I* shouldn't come up here for a few days,' said Jack, finding the idea more and more exciting as he thought about it. 'I could make a hide, you know – and . . .'

'What's a hide?' asked Tassie, speaking for almost the first time that morning.

'A hide? Oh, it's a place I should rig up to hide myself and my camera in,' said Jack. 'Then, when the eagles had got used to it, I could take as many pictures of them as I wanted to, without showing myself or putting them on their guard. I should make my hide somewhere on this crag, within good view of that nest. Golly, I might take a whole set of pictures showing the young eagle learning to fly!'

'Well, ask Mother if you can come up, then,' said Philip. 'I'd come up and be with you, only I think one of us boys ought to be down at the cottage to help bring the wood in for the fire and things like that.'

'I could do that,' said Dinah, eager to get rid of the toad for a few days. She wouldn't go near Philip as long as he had the toad about him.

'Well, you can't,' said Philip. 'Jack will have Kiki for company and we'll come up and see him every day. Come on, now – let's explore the lower parts of the castle a bit more.'

So they made their way back across the yard into the

lower parts of the great building, expecting to see the same vast empty rooms there as they had seen above. But what a surprise they got!

10

A curious thing

They went into a great doorway, and walked across the dark hall, which echoed strangely with their footsteps. From outside came the yelping scream of the eagles again.

'I expect it was the screams of the eagles that the villagers heard year after year up here,' said Jack, as he made his way to a stout door that led off the hall. He opened it – and then stood still in surprise.

This room was furnished! It had once been a kind of sitting room or drawing room, and the mouldy old furniture was still there, though the children could not imagine why it had been left!

They stood and stared into the old, forgotten room in silence. It was such a odd feeling to gaze on this musty-smelling, quiet room, lighted by four slit windows and one wide one, through which sunlight came. It lit up the layers of dust on the sofas and vast table, and touched the enormous webs and hanging cobwebs that were made by scores of busy spiders through the years.

Dinah shivered. When the others went further into the room, walking on tiptoe and talking in whispers, she did not follow. Lucy-Ann patted a chair and at once a cloud of dust arose, making her choke. Philip pulled at a cover on one of the sofas, and it fell to pieces in his hands. It was quite rotten.

'What a weird old room!' he said. 'I feel as if I was back a hundred years or so. Time has stood still here. I do wonder why this room was left like this.'

They went out and into the next one. That was quite empty. But the third one, smaller, and evidently used as a dining-room, was again furnished. And again the spiders' webs stretched everywhere and hung down in long grey threads from the high ceilings. There was a great sideboard in the room, and when the children curiously opened one of the doors, they saw old china and pieces of silver there – or what must have been silver, for now the cruets and sauce-boats were so terribly tarnished that they might have been made of anything.

'Curiouser and curiouser!' said Lucy-Ann, quoting *Alice in Wonderland*. 'Why have these rooms been left like this?'

'I expect the wicked old man Tassie told us about just lived in a few rooms, and these were the ones,' said Jack. 'Mabye he went away, meaning to come back, and never did. And nobody dared to come here – or perhaps nobody even knew the rooms had been left furnished. It's a mystery!'

The little fox cub went sniffing round all the rooms raising clouds of dust, and choking now and again. Kiki did not seem to like the rooms. She stayed on Jack's shoulder quite silent.

They came to the kitchen. This was a simply enormous place, with a great cooking range at the back. Iron sauce-pans and an iron kettle were still there. Philip tried to lift one, but it was immensely heavy.

'Cooks must have had very strong arms in the old days!' he said. 'Look – is that a pump by the old sink? I suppose they had to pump their water up.'

They crossed over to the sink. The old fashioned pump had a handle, which had to be worked up and down in order to bring water from some deep-down well.

Philip stared at it in a puzzled manner, his eyes going to a puddle on the floor, just below the pump.

'What's the matter, Philip?' said Jack.

'Nothing much – but where did that water come from?' said Philip. 'See, it's in a puddle – it can only have been there a day or two, or it would have dried up.'

Jack looked up to the dark old ceiling, as if he expected to see a leak in the roof there. But there was none, of course! He looked down at the puddle again, and he too felt puzzled. 'Let's pump a bit and see if water comes up,' he said, and stretched out his hand. 'Maybe the thing is out of order now.'

Before he could reach the handle Philip knocked his hand aside, with an exclamation. Jack looked at him in surprise.

'See here, Freckles,' said Philip, frowning in bewilderment, 'the handle of the pump isn't covered with dust like everything else is. It's rubbed clean just where you'd take hold of it to pump.'

Dinah felt a little prickle of fright go down her back. Whatever did Philip mean? Who could pump up water in an old empty castle?

They all stared at the pump handle, and saw that Philip was right. Button began to lap up the puddle of water on the stone floor. He was thirsty.

'Wait, Button, I'll pump you some fresh water,' said Philip, and he took hold of the pump handle. He worked it up and down vigorously, and fresh, clear water poured in gushes into the huge old sink. Some of it splashed out into the puddle already on the floor.

'That's how that puddle was made,' said Jack, watching carefully. 'By the splashes of the water from the sink. But that means someone must have pumped up water here in the last few days!'

Tassie's eyes grew big with fright. 'The wicked old man's still here!' she said, and looked fearfully over her shoulder as if she expected him to walk into the kitchen.

'Don't be so silly, Tassie,' said Philip impatiently. 'The old man's dead and gone years and years ago. Do you know if any of the villagers ever come up here?'

'No, oh no!' said Tassie. 'They are afraid of the castle. They say it is a bad place.'

The five children certainly felt that it had a strange, brooding air about it. They felt that they wanted to go out into the sunshine. Kiki suddenly gave a mournful groan that made them all jump.

'Don't, Kiki!' said Jack crossly. 'Philip, what do you make of this? Who's been pumping up the water? Can there be anyone in the castle now?'

'Well, we haven't seen signs of anyone at all,' said Philip. 'And why should anyone be here, anyway? There's nothing for them to live on – no food or anything. I think myself that probably some rambler came up here in curiosity, wandered about, and got himself a drink of water from the pump before he went.'

This seemed the most likely explanation.

'But how did he get in?' said Dinah, after a moment or two.

That was a puzzler. 'There must be some way,' said Jack.

'There isn't,' said Tassie. 'I've been all round the castle, and I know. There isn't any way of getting in.'

'Well, there must be,' said Philip, and dismissed the subject, feeling that they would all be better to be out in the open air, having their tea. 'Come on – let's find a comfortable place in the courtyard and have our tea. I'm jolly hungry again.'

They went into the hot and sunny courtyard. There was little breeze there, for it was enclosed by the high walls. They sat down and Dinah undid the tea packet. There was plenty there for everyone – but all the lemonade had been drunk at dinnertime.

'I'm so thirsty I simply *must* have something to drink with my sandwiches,' said Lucy-Ann. 'My tongue will hang out like a dog's in a minute.'

Everyone felt the same – but nobody particularly wanted to go into that big lonely kitchen and bring back water in the cardboard cups.

'I know – we'll see if the spring that runs down to our cottge is anywhere about,' said Philip. 'It's supposed to begin in this courtyard, I know. It should be somewhere down at the bottom of it.'

He got up and Button went with him. It was Button who found the spring. It gushed out near the wall that ran round the castle, almost at the foot of the tower at the top of which the children had had their dinner. It was not a big spring but the water was cold and clear. Button lapped it eagerly.

Philip filled two cups and called to Jack to bring more. Jack and Tassie came up with the other cups. Jack looked with interest at the bubbling spring. It gushed out from a hole in the rock, and then disappeared again under a tangle of brambles, into a kind of little tunnel that ran below the tower.

'I suppose it goes right underneath the tower, and comes out again further on down the hillside,' thought the boy. 'It collects more and more water on the way, from the inside of the hill, and by the time it reaches Spring Cottage it is quite a big spring, ready to become a proper little stream.'

The children enjoyed the icy-cold water. They finished all the tea, and lay back in the sun, watching the golden eagles, who were once more soaring upwards on wide wings.

'This has been an exciting sort of day,' said Philip lazily. 'What do you feel now about spending a few days here, Jack – won't you be too lonely?'

'I'll have Kiki and the eagles,' said Jack. 'And all the rabbits round about too!'

'I wouldn't like to be here all alone now,' said Dinah. 'Not until I knew who pumped that water! I should feel creepy all the time.'

'That's nothing new,' said Philip. 'You feel creepy if you even see the tip of a worm coming out of a hole. Life must be nothing but creepiness to you. Now if only you'd get used to having toads crawling over you, or a hedgehog in your pocket, or a beetle or two, you'd soon stop feeling creepy.'

'Oh don't!' said Dinah, shivering at the thought of beetles crawling over her. 'You're an awful boy. Jack, you won't really stay here by yourself, will you?'

'I don't see why not,' said Jack, with a laugh. 'I'm not scared. I think Philip's right when he says it was probably only some rambler who pumped himself a spot of water. After all, if we're curious enough to make our way in here other people may be too.'

'Yes, but *how* did they come?' persisted Dinah.

'Same way as old Button came in, I expect,' said Philip.

Dinah stared at him. 'Well – how did *Button* get in?' she said. 'Find out that, and we don't need to use the plank every time!'

'Oh – down a rabbit hole, I should think, and up another,' said Philip, refusing to take her seriously. Dinah gave an angry exclamation.

'Do talk sense! Button could go up a rabbit hole all right, but a man couldn't. You know that quite well.'

'Of course – why didn't I think of that before?' said Philip aggravatingly, and dodged as Dinah threw a clod of earth at him.

'Here! Some of that went in my eye,' said Jack, sitting up. 'Stop it, you two. I know what we'll do. We'll leave old Button behind here when we go across the plank, and we'll watch and see where he comes out. Then we can use his entrance, if it's possible, the next time we come!'

'Yes – that's a good idea,' said Lucy-Ann, and Tassie nodded too. The little girl was puzzled to know how Button had got into the castle. She felt so certain that there was no way in besides the two doors, and the window through which they themselves had come.

'Come on – time to go home,' said Jack, and they all got up. 'I'll be back here tomorrow, I hope!'

11

An unexpected meeting

They went back into the castle and up the wide stone stair. Dinah felt a little uncomfortable and kept close to the others. So did Tassie. They went down the wide corridor and looked into room after room to find the one with the plank.

'Golly! Don't say it's gone!' said Jack, after they had looked into about six rooms. 'This is odd. I'm sure the room wasn't as far along as this.'

But it was – for in the very next room they saw the edge of their plank on the stone sill. They hurried over to it. It was dark in that room. They all wished heartily they had a torch, and determined to bring both torches and candles with them next time!

Jack went across first, with Kiki clutching his shoulder, murmuring something about putting the kettle on. He got across safely, and then caught hold of the rope on the other side. He helped Lucy-Ann across, then Dinah and then Tassie. Lucy-Ann slipped hurriedly down the cliffside, followed by Dinah. Tassie leapt down like a goat, without even touching the rope.

Then came Philip, and poor little Button was left behind, yelping shrilly.

'You go your own way and join us outside the castle!' called back Philip. Button jumped up to the sill but kept falling back. He could not reach it. The children heard him barking away by himself as they made their way down the tunnel-like passage into the sunshine.

'I may have to go back for Button, you know, if he doesn't come after us,' said Philip. 'I couldn't really leave him behind. But foxes are so sharp – I bet he'll come rushing after us in a minute.'

'Keep a good lookout then,' said Jack, 'because we want to know where he gets in and out, so that we can use the place ourselves.'

But it wasn't any good keeping a lookout, for suddenly Button was at their heels, leaping up at Philip, making yelping sounds of happiness and love. Nobody saw him come. Nobody knew how he had got out of the castle!

'How annoying!' said Jack, with a laugh. 'Button, how *did* you get out?'

Button couldn't tell them. He kept so close to Philip's heels all the way home that Philip could feel his sharp little nose the whole time. Button was like a little shadow!

They were all so tired when they got in that they could hardly tell their adventures. When Philip told about the puddle of water below the pump, Mrs Mannering laughed.

'Trust you children to imagine something to scare yourselves with!' she said. 'Probably the pump leaks a bit on its own. It's funny about those old furnished rooms though. It shows how the villagers fear the castle, if no one has interfered with the furniture! Even thieves, apparently, will not venture there.'

Mrs Mannering was intensely interested in the golden eagles. She and Philip and Jack talked about them till darkness fell. Mrs Mannering was quite willing for Jack to try and take pictures of the young eagle with its parents.

'If only you can make a good hide,' she said, 'and get the birds used to it, so that you can lie there and take what pictures you please, it would be marvellous. Philip's father used to do things like that.'

'Can I go with Jack, please Aunty Allie?' asked Lucy-Ann, who couldn't bear to let Jack go off by himself for even a day or two.

'No, you can't, Lucy-Ann,' said Jack decidedly. 'I'm the only one to be there, because if you or the others start messing about too, we shall scare the birds and I shan't get any decent pictures at all. I shan't be gone long! You can't hang on my apron strings *all* the holidays.'

Lucy-Ann said no more. If Jack didn't want her, she wouldn't go.

'You can come up each day and bring me food, if you like,' said Jack, as he saw Lucy-Ann's disappointed face. 'And I can always signal to you from the tower. You know we could see this house from the tower, so, of course, you can see the tower from this house.'

'Oh yes – you signal goodnight to us each night,' said Lucy-Ann, cheering up. 'That would be fun. I wonder which room is best to see the tower from.'

It so happened that it was her own bedroom that was the best. Good! She could even watch the tower from bed. 'Jack, will you sleep in the tower?' she said. 'Then I shall look at the tower when I wake, and know you're there. I'll wave a white hanky from my window when I see you waving one.'

'Oh – I don't know where I'll sleep,' said Jack. 'The tower would be too draughty. I'll curl myself up in the rug in a warm corner somewhere – or maybe clear a place on one of those big old couches. If I can get the dust off!'

Tassie couldn't imagine how anyone could possibly dare to sleep alone in the old castle. She thought Jack must be the bravest boy in the world.

'Time for you to go home, Tassie,' said Mrs Mannering. 'Go along. You can come back tomorrow.'

Tassie disappeared, running off to her tumbledown cottage and her scolding, untidy mother. The others helped Mrs Mannering to clear the supper away, and the two girls washed up, half asleep.

They went to bed, to dream of the old deserted castle, of strange cobwebby rooms, high towers, screaming eagles – and a puddle on the floor below the pump!

'That's really a puzzle,' said Philip to himself, as he fell asleep. 'But I'm too tired to think about it now!'

The next day was rainy. Great clouds swept over the hillside, making it misty and damp. The sun hardly showed all day long. The little spring suddenly became twice as full, and made quite a noise as it gurgled down the garden.

'Blow!' said Jack. 'I did want to go up to the castle today. I feel that that young eagle may fly at any time now, and I don't want to miss its first flight.'

'Have you got plenty of films for your camera?' asked Philip. 'You know how you keep running out of them just when you badly want them.'

'Well, it wouldn't be much good wanting them if I *hadn't* got enough!' said Jack. 'I couldn't buy them in that tiny village. There's only one shop.'

'You could take the train and go off to the nearest big town,' said Mrs Mannering. 'Why don't you do that, instead of staying here cooped up all day? I can see Dinah is longing to squabble with someone!'

Dinah laughed. She did hate being 'cooped up' as Mrs Mannering said, and it did make her irritable. But Dinah was learning to control herself a little more now that she was growing older.

'Yes, it would be fun to take the train and go off shopping,' she said. 'Let's do it! We've just got time to catch the one and only train that leaves the station, and we'll come back by the one and only train that returns!'

So they put on macks and sou'westers and hurried to catch the train. But they needn't have hurried, really, for the leisurely little country train always waited for anybody coming along the road.

It was twenty miles to the nearest town. It took the train a whole hour to get there, and the children enjoyed running through the valleys in between the ranges of high hills. Once they saw another castle on the side of a hill, but they all agreed that it wasn't a patch on theirs.

Button had been left behind with Tassie, much to his dismay. The children had offered to take Tassie with them, but the little girl was terrified of the train. She shrank back when they suggested it. So they gave Button to her with strict injunctions not to let him worry Mrs Mannering.

Kiki, of course, went with Jack. But then she went everywhere with him, making her remarks, and causing a great deal of amusement and interest. She always showed off in company and sometimes became very cheeky.

The children had left the train and were walking down the street, when suddenly a voice hailed them, and made them jump. 'Hallo, hallo! Whoever would have thought of seeing *you* here!'

The children turned round at once and Kiki let out a delighted squawk.

'Bill Smugs!' cried the children, and ran to the ruddy-faced, twinkling-eyed man who had hailed them. Lucy-Ann gave him a hug, Dinah smiled in delight, and the two boys banged Bill Smugs on the back.

Bill Smugs was not his real name. It was a name he had told the children the year before, when they had come across him trying to track some clever forgers. He had not wanted them to know who he was nor what he was really doing – but although they now knew his real name, he was still Bill Smugs to them, and always would be.

'Come and have lunch with me,' said Bill Smugs. 'Or have you any other plans? I really must know what you are doing here. I thought you were at home for the holidays.'

'What are *you* doing here?' asked Philip, his eyes shining.

'On the track of forgers again? I bet you're on some sort of exciting job.'

'Maybe, maybe not,' said Bill, smiling. 'I shouldn't tell you, anyway, should I? I'm probably holidaying, just as you are. Come on – we'll go to this hotel. It looks about the best one this town can produce.'

It was an exciting lunch. Bill Smugs was an exciting person. They talked eagerly about the thrilling adventure he had had with them the year before, when they had all got mixed up with copper mines and forgers, and had been in very great danger. They reminded each other of the times they had shivered and trembled!

'Yes, that certainly was an adventure,' said Bill, helping himself to apple tart and ice cream. 'And now, as I said before – you really must tell me what you are doing in this part of the world!'

The children told him, interrupting each other in their eagerness, especially Jack, who was longing to tell him every detail about the eagles. Bill listened and ate solidly, giving Kiki titbits every now and again. She had been delighted to see their old friend too, and had told him at least a dozen times to open his book at page six, and pay attention.

'What a pity you're twenty miles away or more,' said Bill. 'I'm stuck here in this district for a time, I'm afraid, and can't leave. But if I can I'll come over and see you. Maybe your mother would put me up for a day or two, then I can come up to this wonderful castle of yours and see the eagles.'

'Oh yes, *do* come!' they all cried. 'We aren't on the telephone,' added Philip, 'but never mind, just come – we are sure to be there. Come at any time! We'd love you to.'

'Right,' said Bill. 'I might be able to slip over next week, because it doesn't look as if I'm going to do much good here. Can't tell you any more, I'm afraid – but if I don't make any headway with what I'm supposed to be doing, I'll have a break, and come along to see you and your nice mother. Give her my kind regards, and say Bill Smugs will come and pay his repects if he possibly can.'

'We'll have to go,' said Jack regretfully, looking at his watch. 'There's only the one train back and we've got a bit of shopping to do. Goodbye, Bill, it's been grand to bump into you like this.'

'Goodbye. See you soon, I hope!' said Bill, with his familiar grin. And off they ran to catch their train.

12

Jack is left at the castle

Mrs Mannering was delighted to hear that they had by chance met Bill Smugs again, for she felt very grateful to him for the help he had given the children in their amazing adventure the year before.

'If he comes, I will sleep in with you girls and he can have my room,' she said. 'Good old Bill! It will be nice to see him again. He must lead an interesting life, always hunting down criminal and wicked people.'

'I bet he'd have been after the wicked old man who used to live in the castle!' said Lucy-Ann. 'It will be fun to take him up there. Jack, I hope it won't be raining tomorrow again.'

But it was. Jack felt very disappointed. He was afraid that the old eagle might take the young one away. But it was no good going up the hill in this pouring rain. For one thing, the clouds were so low that they sailed round the hillside itself, big patches of moving mist. He would get lost if he tried to go up.

'I suppose Tassie could find her way up even in the mist,'

he said. Tassie was there. She raised her bright black eyes to him and nodded.

Yes,' she said. 'I will take you now if you like.'

'No,' said Mrs Mannering firmly. 'Wait till tomorrow. I think it will be fine then. I'm not going to have to send out search-parties for you and Tassie!'

'But, Mother, Tassie could find her way up this hillside blindfold, I'm sure she could!' said Philip. However, Mrs Mannering didn't believe in Tassie and her powers as much as the children did. So Jack had to wait for the next day.

Luckily it was fine. The sun rose out of a clear sky, and not even the smallest cloud showed itself. The hillside glistened and gleamed as the sun dried the millions of raindrops left on twig and leaf. It was a really lovely day.

'We'll all come up with you, Jack,' said Philip, 'and help to carry what you want. You'll need a couple of thick rugs, and some food – a candle or two and a torch – and your camera and films, of course.'

They all decided to have a day up at the castle again, and leave Jack behind when they came back in the evening. So, about eleven o'clock, with the morning sun blazing hotly down on their backs, they began the climb up the hill.

Button came, of course, and Kiki. Kiki was to stay with Jack. The eagles evidently didn't mind her. In fact it was quite possible that they might make friends with her, and Jack might get some interesting photographs.

Carrying various things, the little party set off once more. Dinah was glad to feel her torch safely in her pocket. She didn't mean to stand in dark rooms again and feel cobwebs clutching at her hair!

They climbed in through the window as before. Button again appeared in the courtyard from somewhere, though still no one knew where. Kiki flew to the crag on which the eagles had their nest, yelping her eagle scream in what was plainly meant to be a kindly greeting.

The startled eagles rose up in surprise, and then seeing the stange and talkative bird again, circled round her. Quite clearly they didn't mind her in the least. They probably took her to be some sort of strange eagle cousin, as she spoke their language!

It wasn't long before Jack climbed up to see if the young eagle was still in the nest. It was! The mother had just brought it a dead rabbit, and the young eagle was busy on the meal. When it saw Jack it stood over the rabbit with wings held over it, as if afraid that Jack would take it.

'It's all right,' said the boy gently. 'Eat it all. I don't want any. I only want a picture of you!'

He looked around for a place to make a good hide in. There was one spot that looked ideal. It was a thick gorse-bush, almost on a level with the eagles' ledge. Jack thought he could probably squeeze into the hollow middle of it, and make an opening for his camera in the prickly branches.

'The only thing is – I'll get terribly pricked,' he thought. 'Never mind. It will be worth it if I get some good pictures! I bet the eagles will never know whether I'm hiding in that bush or not!'

He told the others, and they agreed with him that it would be a splendid place, if a bit painful. The bush was quite hollow in the middle, and once he was there he could manage not to be pricked. It was the getting in and out that would be unpleasant.

'You'll have to wrap this rug round you,' said Lucy-Ann, holding up the thick rug she had brought. 'If you creep in with this round you, you'll be all right.'

'Good idea,' said Jack.

They went up to the tower-top and had their dinner there again, seeing the countryside spread out below once more in all its beauty.

'I'd like Bill Smugs to see this,' said Jack. 'We must bring him up here when he comes.'

'Where do you think you will sleep tonight, Jack?' asked Lucy-Ann anxiously. 'And will you wave your hanky from the tower before you go to sleep? I'll watch for it.'

'I'll wave my white shirt,' said Jack. 'You probably wouldn't notice anything so small as a hanky, though you can borrow my old fieldglasses and look through them, if you like. They're in my room.'

'Oh yes, I will,' said Lucy-Ann. 'I shall easily see your shirt. I hope you won't be too lonely, Jack.'

''Course not. I'll have Kiki. Nobody could possibly be lonely with that old chatterbox of a bird,' said Jack, scratching Kiki's feathered poll.

'Pop goes the weasel,' said Kiki, and nibbled at Jack's ear.

'You haven't said where you'll sleep, Jack,' said Lucy-Ann. 'You won't really sleep on one of those old sofas, will you?'

'No, I don't think so. More likely in a sandy corner of the courtyard,' said Jack. 'There's a sandy bit over there, look – it'll be warm with the sun. If I curl up there and wrap the rugs all round me, I'll be very snug.'

'I'd rather you slept out in the courtyard somehow, than in the strange old castle!' said Lucy-Ann. 'I don't like those musty, dusty, fusty rooms!'

'Musty, dusty, fusty!' sang Kiki, delighted. 'Musty, fusty, dusty, musty, fusty . . .'

'Shut up, Kiki,' said everyone; but Kiki loved those three words, and went to repeat them over and over again to Button, who sat listening, his ears cocked, and his little foxy head on one side.

'It's time for us to go,' said Philip at last. They had tried in vain to find the place where Button had got in and out, and had wandered once more all over the castle, switching on their torches, and exploring even more thoroughly than before. Only the three rooms they had seen before were furnished – the sitting room, the dining room and the kitchen. There was no bedroom furnished, which, as Philip pointed out, was rather a pity, as Jack could probably have made himself comfortable in a big old four poster bed!

Jack said goodbye to them all as they went across the plank. He held Button in his arms, quite determined to follow him and find out where he went, when he got out of the castle. He was not going to set him free till the others had gone. One by one they crossed the plank and disappeared. Their voices died away. Jack was alone.

He went down the wide corridor, down the stone stairway that led to the dark hall, and out into the courtyard, where the last rays of the sun still shone. When he came to the yard, he set the wriggling fox cub down.

'Now you show me where you go,' he said. Button darted off at once – far too quickly for Jack! By the time the boy had run a few steps after him, the fox cub had disappeared, and there was no trace of him.

'Blow!' said Jack, annoyed. 'I did mean to discover the way out you went, this time – but you're so jolly nippy! I suppose you have already joined the others now.'

Jack went to try and arrange his camera safely in the gorse bush. He had a very good camera indeed, given to him last Christmas by Bill Smugs. In his pocket were many rolls of film. He ought to be able to take a fine series of pictures of those eagles.

He wrapped one of the rugs round him, as Lucy-Ann had suggested, and began to squeeze through the prickly branches. Some of the prickles reached his flesh even through the thick rug. Kiki sat beside the bush, watching Jack in surprise.

'What a pity, what a pity, what a pity!' she said.

'It *is* a pity that I'm being pricked like this!' groaned Jack. But he cheered up when he saw what a fine view of the eagles' nest he had – and of the ledge where the eagles sat to look out at the surrounding country. The distance was perfect, and Jack rejoiced.

By making an opening in the bush on the side where the nest was, he managed to point his camera in exactly the right direction, and lodged it very firmly on its tripod legs. He looked through it to see what kind of a picture he would get.

'Perfect!' thought the boy joyfully. 'I won't take one now, because the light is awkward. But tomorrow morning would be exactly right. Then the sun will be just where I want it.'

The little eagle caught sight of the camera peering out of the bush. It did not like it. It cowered down in the nest, afraid.

'You'll soon get used to it,' Jack thought. 'I hope the old birds will too. Oh, Kiki, did you *have* to get into the middle of the bush too? There's really only just room enough for me!'

'Fusty, musty, dusty!' whispered Kiki, evidently thinking that Jack was playing a game of hide-and-seek with somebody and mustn't be given away. 'Fusty, musty, dusty.'

'Silly old bird,' said Jack. 'Now get out, please. I'm coming out too. It's certainly fusty and musty in this gorse-bush, even if it isn't dusty!'

Kiki crawled out and then Jack forced his way out, trying to protect himself from the prickly stems. He stood up, stretched himself, took the rug and went down the crag lightly, leaving his camera in position. It was clear that there would be no rain that night!

The boy read a book until daylight faded. Then he remembered about waving his shirt from the tower. So up he went, hoping he hadn't left it too late for Lucy-Ann to see.

He stood on the top of the tower, and stripped off his white shirt. Then he waved it gaily in the strong breeze there, looking down on the cottage far below as he waved. And from the topmost window there came a flash of white.

Lucy-Ann was waving back.

'He's just waved,' she called to Dinah, who was undressing. 'I saw the white shirt. Good. Now I know he's all right and will soon be curling himself up to go to sleep.'

'Why you must fuss so about Jack I don't know,' said Dinah, jumping into bed. 'I never fuss about Philip. You're silly, Lucy-Ann.'

'I don't care,' thought Lucy-Ann, as she settled down in bed. 'I'm glad to know Jack is safe. Somehow I don't like him being all alone in that horrid old castle!'

13

Noises in the night

Jack went down the stone stairways of the tower, whistling softly. Kiki whistled with him. If it was a tune she knew, she would whistle it all through with Jack.

They came into the old courtyard. There was no sign of the eagles. They were probably roosting now. But, at Jack's coming, there was a general scurrying all around the yard.

'Rabbits!' said Jack, in delight. 'Golly, what hundreds of them! I suppose they all come out this time of the evening. I'll curl myself up in that sandy corner and watch them for a bit. Now, don't you frighten them, Kiki.'

He went over to the soft sand, taking with him the thick rugs and a packet of chocolate biscuits. He curled himself up, and lay there, watching the rabbits creeping out of their holes again.

It was a lovely sight to see. There were big ones and little ones, dark ones and light ones and playful ones. Some nibbled patches of wiry grass here and there. Others leapt about madly.

Jack lay there contentedly and nibbled his biscuits, enjoying the chocolate on them. He watched the rabbits in delight. Kiki watched them too, murmuring a few remarks into Jack's ear now and again.

'I bet the eagles catch a good few of those rabbits,' thought Jack, suddenly feeling sleepy. He finished his last biscuit, and pulled the rugs more closely around him. He felt a little chilly now. The sand didn't feel quite so soft as it had done before, either. Jack hoped he wasn't going to be uncomfortable. Perhaps it would have been better to have chosen a patch of heather.

'Well, I'm too sleepy to change my bed now,' he thought. 'Much too sleepy. Kiki, move up a bit. Your claws are digging into my neck. You'd better get off me and perch somewhere else.'

But before Kiki could move, Jack was asleep. Kiki stayed where she was. The rabbits grew bolder and played nearer to the sleeping boy. A half-moon came out of the evening clouds and lighted up the dreaming courtyard.

What woke Jack he never knew. But something woke him with a jump. He opened his eyes and lay there, looking up into the night sky, full of surprise. For a moment or two he had no idea where he was.

Usually when he woke he saw the ceiling of his room – now there were stars and clouds. Then he suddenly remembered. Of course – he was in the courtyard of the old castle. He sat up and Kiki awoke too, giving an annoyed little squawk.

'I wonder what woke me?' thought Jack, looking round the shadowy yard. The moon came out again and he saw a few rabbits here and there. Behind rose the great dark bulk of the castle.

Jack felt absolutely certain that something had awakened him. Some noise perhaps? Or had a rabbit run over him? He listened intently, but he could hear nothing save the hoot of an owl on the hillside: 'Hoo-hoo-hoo-hoo! Hoo-hoo-hoo-hoo!' Then he heard the high squeak of a bat, catching beetles in the night air.

He glanced up at the tower from which he had waved his white shirt – and he suddenly stiffened in surprise. Surely that was a light he saw flash there?

He stared intently, waiting for it to come again. It had seemed rather like the sudden flash of a torch. But it didn't come again.

Jack sat and thought hard. Was it a flash? Had someone walked along the battlemented wall to the tower, and was it their footsteps that awakened him? *Was* there someone in the castle after all?

It seemed rather weird. Jack wondered what to do. He didn't really feel inclined to get up and find out what the flash was – if it *had* been a flash. He was beginning to doubt that it was now. If only if would come again, he would know.

He decided that it was cowardly to stay in his bed just because he felt a bit scared. He had better get up and make his way to the tower to see if anyone was there. That would be the brave thing to do.

'I don't feel at all brave,' thought Jack, 'but I suppose a person is really bravest when he does something although he is frightened. So here goes!'

Warning Kiki to be quite quiet, he made his way very carefully across the yard to the entrance of the castle, keeping in the blackest shadows. The feel of Kiki's feet on his shoulder was somehow very comforting.

He went into the vast hall and listened. There was not a sound to be heard. He switched on his torch, cautiously covering it with his handkerchief. The hall was empty. Jack went up the wide stone stairway, and found his way to the wall that led to the tower. He walked quietly along it keeping close to one edge, and soon came to the tower.

'Shall I go up or not?' wondered the boy. 'I don't want to in the least. If there's anyone there they can't be up to any good. *Did* I imagine that flash?'

He screwed up his courage and stole up the tower stairway. There was no one in the tower room. He crept up the stairway that led to the very top, and put his head carefully out. The moon's light was enough to show him that there was nobody there either.

'Well – I just must have imagined it,' thought the boy. 'How silly of me! I'll go back to bed again.'

Down he went once more Kiki still on his shoulder. As he came into the wide hall, he suddenly stopped still. He had heard a sound. What could it be?

It sounded like a muffled clanking – and then surely that was the splash of water?

'Is it somebody in the kitchen – somebody getting a drink of water again?' wondered Jack, feeling a prickle of panic go down his back. 'Golly, I don't like this. I wish the others were here.'

He stood quite still, wondering what to do. Then, overcome by fear, he fled out of the hall and into the moonlight yard, keeping in the shadows. He was trembling. Kiki bent to his ear, murmuring something supposed to be comforting. She knew he was frightened.

In a minute or two he was ashamed of himself. 'Why am I running away?' he thought. 'This won't do. Just to show myself that I'm no coward I'll walk into that kitchen and see who's there! It's a tramp, I expect, who knows the way in. He'll be far more frightened to see me than I shall be to see him!'

Boldly, but very quickly, the boy went back into the dark, brooding castle. Through the hall he went, and made his way softly to the kitchen entrance. He slipped inside the doorway, and then went behind the door, where he waited, listening and watching to see if any light was shown.

But there was dead silence. There was no clank of the pump. There was no splash of water. Jack waited for two or three minutes, with Kiki, perfectly silent.

He could not even hear anyone breathing. The kitchen must be empty.

'I'll switch on my torch very quickly, flash it round the kitchen, and see if there's anyone standing quietly there,' he thought. 'I can easily run out of the door if there is.'

So he took his torch from his pocket, and suddenly pressed down the switch. He flashed it to the sink, where the pump stood. There was no one there. He flashed it all round the kitchen. It was quite empty. There was no sign of anyone at all.

Jack heaved a sigh of relief. He went across to the sink and examined the floor beside it. There was again a puddle there – but was it a freshly-made one from the sink splashes – or was it the same one they themselves had made when they used the pump?

Jack couldn't tell. He looked closely at the pump, but that told him nothing, of course.

'It's a puzzle,' Jack said to Kiki, in a whisper. 'I suppose the clank and the splashing were all my silly imagination. I was frightened, and people always imagine things then. I imagined that flash in the tower, and I imagined the clanking noise and the splashing. Kiki, I'm as timid as Lucy-Ann – I really am.'

Still feeling a bit puzzled, but rather ashamed of all his fears and alarms, Jack went back to his bed in the courtyard.

It seemed uncomfortably hard now. Also he was a bit cold. He pulled the rugs round him and tried to get comfortable. He shut his eyes and told himself to go to sleep. The moon seemed to have gone now, and everything was pitch-black. Whatever he heard or saw, Jack was determined he was not going to leave his bed again that night. Let people flash lights all they liked, and pump water all night long if they wanted to! *He* wouldn't bother about it!

He was wide awake. He simply couldn't go to sleep. He didn't feel frightened any more. He only felt annoyed because sleep wouldn't come to him. He began to think about his eagles, and planned some fine camera work for the next day.

He could feel Kiki perched on his shoulderbone. He knew she had her head under her wing, and was sleeping. He wished she was awake and would talk to him. He wished the other children were with him. Then he could tell them what he had imagined he saw and heard.

At last he fell asleep, just as the dawn was making the eastern sky silvery. He didn't see it turn gold and pink, nor did he see the first soaring flight of the two eagles. He slept soundly, and so did Kiki. But she awoke at the first yelping scream of one of the eagles, and answered it with one of her marvellous imitations.

That woke Jack with a jump, and he sat up. Kiki flew off his shoulder, waited till he called her, and flew back again. Jack rubbed his eyes and yawned.

'I'm hungry,' he said to Kiki. 'Are you?'

'Fusty, musty, dusty,' said Kiki, remembering the three words she had so much liked the day before. 'Fusty, mus . . .'

'Yes, I heard you the first time,' said Jack. 'I say, Kiki, do you remember how we got up in the middle of the night and went to the tower and to the kitchen?'

Kiki apparently did. She scratched her beak with one of her feet and looked at Jack. 'What a pity, what a pity!' she remarked.

'Yes – I think it *was* a pity we disturbed ourselves so much,' said Jack. 'I was an idiot, Kiki. Now that it's broad daylight, and I'm wide awake, I begin to think I must have dreamt or imagined all that happened in the night – not that anything much did happen, anyway.'

Kiki listened with her head on one side. Jack unwrapped himself from the rug. 'I tell you what, Kiki – we won't either of us mention that flash in the tower, or the mysterious clanking or splashing we thought we heard, see? The others would only laugh at us – and Lucy-Ann and Tassie might be frightened. I'm sure it was all my imagination.'

Kiki appeared to agree with every word. She helped Jack to get biscuits out of a packet, and fruit out of a bag, and watched him take the top off a bottle of ginger beer.

'I wonder what time the others will be up,' said Jack, beginning his breakfast. 'We'll try and take a few pictures before they come, shall we, Kiki?'

14

Jack gets a shock

After he had had his breakfast Jack went to his hide. It was a lovely day. He could take some fine pictures if only the eagles were there.

He wrapped the thickest rug round him and crawled in through the prickly stems of the gorse. Kiki remained outside this time.

When he was in the hollow centre of the bush Jack examined his camera to make sure that it was all right. It was. He looked through the shutter to see if he had it trained exactly on the nest.

'Perfect!' he thought. 'That young eagle appears to be asleep. I might get a good picture when it wakes up. I suppose the other birds are soaring miles high into the sky.'

It was boring, waiting for the eagle to wake up. But Jack didn't mind. Both he and Philip knew that the ability to keep absolutely still and silent for a long time on end was essential to the study of birds and animals in their natural surroundings. So Jack settled back in the gorse bush, and waited.

Kiki went off on errands of her own. She flew to the top of the nearest tower and looked down on the countryside. She flew down to the courtyard and looked inside a paper bag there, hoping to find a forgotten biscuit. She sat on the branch of a birch tree, practising quietly to herself the barking noise that Button the fox cub made. So long as Jack was somewhere near she was happy. He was safe in that gorse bush. Kiki didn't know why he had chosen such a peculiar resting place, but Jack was always wise in her eyes.

The young eagle suddenly awoke and stretched out first one wing and then another. It climbed to the edge of the nest and looked out over the ledge, waiting for its parents to come back.

'Fine!' whispered Jack, and pressed the trigger of the camera to take the eagle's picture. The young bird heard the click and cowered down at once – but the snap had been taken!

Soon the bird recovered from its fright and climbed up again. Then, with yelps, the two grown eagles came gliding down on outspread wings, and the young one greeted them gladly, spreading out its wings and quivering them.

One of the eagles had a young hare clutched in its claws. It dropped it into the nest. At once the youngster covered the food with its big wings, cowered over it, and began to pull at it hungrily with its powerful beak.

Jack snapped it. All three birds heard the click and looked towards the gorse bush suspiciously. The male eagle glared and Jack felt uncomfortable. He hoped the bird wouldn't pounce at the gleaming camera lens and ambush it.

But Kiki saved the situation by flying down in a most comradely manner to the eagles, and saluting them in their own yelping language.

They appeared to be quite pleased to see her again

although the young eagle covered the dead hare threateningly with its wings as if to keep Kiki off.

'Open your books at page six,' said Kiki pleasantly. The eagles looked startled. They had not yet got used to the parrot talking in human language. She barked like Button, and they looked rather alarmed.

The female eagle bent herself forward, opened her cruel beak, and made a curious snarling noise, warning Kiki to be careful. She at once spoke in eagle language again, and gave such a fine scream that both eagles were satisfied. The young one fell upon its meal and ate till it could eat no more. Then it sank back into the big nest.

The female eagle finished the dead hare in a very short while. Jack got another wonderful snap whilst it was tearing up its food.

This time, except for an enquiring look in the direction of the click, the eagles took no notice.

'Good,' thought Jack. 'They won't mind the click soon or the gleaming eye of the camera!'

He spent a pleasant morning, using up the rest of his film, delighted to think of the wonderful pictures he could develop. He imagined them in nature magazines, with his name under them as photographer. How proud he would feel!

Kiki suddenly gave a most excited squawk, making the two grown eagles rise in the air in alarm. She flew into the air, and made for the wall that ran round the courtyard. Jack, peering through the back of his hiding-place, saw her fly right over the wall, and disappear.

'Now where's she gone?' he thought. 'I was just going to take a picture of her and the two eagles together.'

Kiki was gone for about half an hour before Jack saw her again. Then she came into the courtyard on Tassie's shoulder! She had heard the other children coming up the hillside and had flown to meet them. They had got into the castle in the usual way, and were now looking for Jack.

The eagles soared into the air when they heard the children coming towards their crag. Jack gave a hail from the inside of his hide.

'I'm here! Hallo, it's good to see you. Wait a sec and I'll be out.'

He crawled out with the rug round him and went down to the others. Lucy-Ann eyed him anxiously, and was relieved to see him looking cheerful and well. So he hadn't minded his lonely night at the castle after all.

'We've brought a fine dinner,' said Philip. 'Mother managed to get some cooked ham and a big fruit cake in the village.'

'Good!' said Jack, realising that he was terribly hungry. 'I've only had biscuits and fruit for my breakfast, washed down with ginger beer.'

'We've got some more ginger beer too,' said Dinah. 'Where shall we have our dinner? On the top of the tower again or where?'

'Here, I think,' said Jack, 'because the light is perfect for taking pictures this morning, and if those eagles come back I want a few more snaps of them. I've an idea they are going to make that young one fly soon. The female eagle tried to tip it off the edge of the nest this morning.'

'Kiki came to meet us,' said Tassie. 'Did you see how Button came in this morning, Jack? We left him outside, but he's here again.'

'No, I didn't,' said Jack. 'I can't see much from the inside of that gorse bush, you know. We shall never find out how Button gets in – I bet it's down an old rabbit hole. He won't be able to do that when he gets a bit bigger. Has he been good?'

'Not very,' said Philip. 'He somehow got into the larder and gobbled up all Mother's sausages. She wasn't at all pleased. I can't imagine how he can eat anything else at the moment. He must have eaten a pound and a half of sausages.'

'Greedy pig.' said Jack, giving Button half his ham sandwich. 'You don't deserve this but you're so sweet I can't help spoiling you.'

'It's a pity he smells so strong,' said Dinah, wrinkling up her nose. 'You won't be able to keep him when he's grown a bit more, Philip – he'll smell too much.'

'That's all *you* know!' said Philip. 'I shall probably keep him till he dies of old age.'

'Well, you'll have to wear a gas mask then,' said Jack, grinning. 'Another sandwich, please, Dinah. Golly, these are good.'

'What sort of a night did you have, Jack?' asked Lucy-Ann, who was sitting as close to Jack as she could.

'Oh, very good,' said Jack airily. 'I woke up once and took some time to go to sleep again.'

He was determined not to say anything about his alarms and fears in the night. They seemed so silly now, in the full sunshine with people all round him.

'You should have seen the rabbits in the late evening,' he said to Philip. 'You'd have loved them. They wouldn't come to me of course, but I daresay you'd have got them all over you! They seemed as tame as anything.'

The four children stayed with Jack till after tea. Each crept into his hide to watch the eagles. They went up to the tower again, and Jack cautiously looked round to see if there was anything different about the tower – a cigarette end, a scrap of paper – but there was nothing at all.

'Won't you come back with us tonight, Jack?' asked Lucy-Ann.

'Of course not,' said Jack, though secretly he felt that he *would* rather like to. 'Is it likely, just as I'm certain that young eagle is going to learn to fly?'

'All right,' said Lucy-Ann, with a sigh, 'I don't know why

I hate you being here alone in this horrid old castle, but I just do.'

'It's not a horrid castle,' said Jack. 'It's just old and forgotten, but it's not horrid.'

'Well, *I* think it is,' said Lucy-Ann. 'I think horrid, wicked things have been done here in the past – and I think they might be done again in the future.'

'You're just dreaming,' said Jack, 'and you're frightening poor Tassie. It's only an old empty place forgotten for years, with nobody in it at all except me and the eagles, bats and rabbits.'

'It's time to go,' said Philip, getting up. 'We brought you another rug, Jack, in case you felt cold. Coming to see us off at the window?'

'Yes, of course,' said Jack, and they all went inside the castle, their footsteps echoing on the stone floor. They went to the room where the plank reached to the windowsill, and one by one they got across.

Lucy-Ann called a farewell to Jack.

'Thank you for waving your shirt to me last night!' she called. 'And oh, Jack I saw you flashing your torch from the tower later on, too! I was in bed, but I was awake and I saw the flash of the torch three or four times. It was nice of you to do that. I was glad to see it and to know you were awake too!'

'Come on, Lucy-Ann, for goodness' sake!' called Dinah. 'You know Mother said we weren't to be late tonight.'

'All right, I'm coming,' said Lucy-Ann, and slid down the creepers to the ground. Everyone called goodbye and then they were gone.

But Jack was left feeling most puzzled and uncomfortable! So there *had* been someone in the tower last night flashing a torch! He hadn't dreamt it or imagined it. It was true.

'Lucy-Ann saw it, so that proves I wasn't mistaken as I

thought,' said the boy to himself as he went back to the courtyard. 'It's terribly mysterious. That clanking I heard and the splashing must have been real too. There *is* someone else here – but who – and why?'

He wished now that he had told the others the happenings in the night. But it was too late, they were gone. Jack now longed to be gone with them! Suppose he heard noises again and saw flashes? He didn't like it. It was weird and eerie and altogether unpleasant.

'Shall I go after the others and join them?' he thought. 'No, I won't. I'll wait and try and find out who's here. Fancy Lucy-Ann seeing those flashes! I *am* glad she told me!'

15

The hidden room

Jack wandered back to his hide. He felt safe there. He was sure no one would ever think of looking in the very middle of a prickly, thick gorse bush for anyone. As evening fell he felt sleepy. Should he try and go to sleep now, and keep awake later on? Could he possibly go to sleep in the hollow gorse bush?

He curled up in the thickest rug and made a pillow of another one. Kiki crawled in beside him and perched uncomfortably on his knees, her head bent to avoid a prickly bit of gorse. The eagles were not to be seen. The young one was down in the nest. Anyway, the light was now too bad to bother about photographs.

Jack managed to fall asleep. He snored a little, for he had his head in an uncomfortable position. Kiki imitated the snore perfectly for a little while, and then, as Jack made no remark about it to her, put her head under her wing and slept too.

Jack slept till midnight. Then he awoke suddenly, feeling dreadfully uncomfortable. He stretched out, wondering where he was, and was immediately and painfully pricked by the gorse. He drew his legs in again hastily.

'I'm in the gorse bush, of course,' he said to himself. 'I must have been asleep for ages. What's the time?'

He looked at the phosporescent hands of his watch and saw that it was ten past midnight.

'Hm,' said Jack, 'Just about the time that someone in the castle starts to wake up! I suppose, if I am going to do any tracking, I'd better get out of here and watch and listen.'

He crept painfully out of the bush, disturbing Kiki, who protested loudly till he made her be silent. 'I'll leave you behind if you make a row like that!' whispered Jack furiously. Kiki fell silent. She always knew when Jack wanted her to be quiet.

Now he was out of the bush, climbing silently down the crag, glad of the faint light of the moon, now a little bigger than the night before. He came into the yard and stood listening.

There was no sound to be heard except the wind blowing fairly hard. And then Jack thought he heard the far off sound of water splashing again – and the clank of the pump handle!

He stood listening. After a while he felt sure he heard quiet footsteps on stone somewhere – was it someone walking on the castle wall – going to the tower to flash a torch again?

'Well, if he's gone to the tower, he's safely out of the castle,' thought Jack. 'I'll go in and see if I can discover any signs of him – where he hides, for instance. He must live somewhere! But it didn't look as if anyone had gone into any of those furnished rooms in the castle. So where in the world does he hide? And what about food? Gosh, it's a mystery!'

The boy stole quietly into the castle, Kiki on his shoulder. He was too excited to feel frightened tonight. Now that he was certain someone else was in the castle besides himself he was too anxious to find out about them to feel any real fears.

He went into the hall of the castle – and at once something struck him with surprise – there was a light coming from somewhere! A dim light certainly, but a light. Jack stared round him, puzzled.

Then he saw where it came from. It came from the floor – or rather, underneath the floor of the hall! The boy stepped forward cautiously. He came to a hole in the floor of the hall – there was no trap-door; it looked exactly like a hole, and yet Jack was sure it had never been there before – and up from this hole came the light.

Jack looked down. Stone steps went down into whatever was below – cellar or dungeon, he didn't know. He ran swiftly to the front entrance of the castle to see if anyone was in the tower. If there was, there would be time for him to slip down the steps and explore.

He saw a flash from the tower. Good. Whoever was there was signalling again. It would be a minute or two before they came back. There would be time to explore this curious opening. In a flash Jack was down the stone steps and then looked around him in the very greatest surprise.

He seemed to be in a kind of museum! He was in a large, underground room, with tapestries on the stone walls, and a thick covering on the floor. Round the room stood suits of armour, just as there often is in a museum. Old heavy chairs stood here and there, and a long narrow table, with crockery and glass on it, ran the length of the room.

Jack stared round in the utmost astonishment. Everything was old – but it was plain that this room was not neglected and deserted as the other furnished rooms were. There were no cobwebs here, no dust.

In the corner was a big old four-poster bed, hung with heavy tapestries. Jack went over to it. It had obviously been slept in, for the pillows were dented, and the sheets hurriedly thrown back as if someone had leapt out in a hurry.

There was a pitcher of ice-cold water on the table. 'Got from the pump, I suppose!' thought Jack. 'So that's why there are always puddles on the floor there. Someone goes for water each night.'

Kiki flew to a suit of armour and stood on the helmet, looking in through the visor as if she expected to glimpse someone inside. Jack giggled a little. Evidently Kiki thought the suits of armour were real peopole and couldn't understand them at all.

At this moment he thought he heard a noise, and in sudden fright he darted up the stone steps to the top, taking Kiki with him. He hopped out just in time, and fled to the dark shadows at the back of the hall. Then, fearing that the person whose footsteps he heard might see him by the light of the torch he was using, he went into one of the furnished rooms – the old drawing-room.

But in going inside he fell over a stool and came to the ground. The footsteps outside stopped suddenly. The torch-light went out. Evidently the person was standing perfectly still and listening hard. He had heard the noise.

With his heart beating fast Jack slipped round the corner of an old couch, and knelt there, with Kiki on his shoulder. Both were as quiet as they could be, but Jack couldn't help feeling certain that the man who was listening must be able to hear the beating of his heart!

The boy heard a cautious footstep coming into the room. Then there was silence again. Then another footstep sounded, a little nearer. Jack's hair began to prickle on his scalp and stand up straight. If the man came round the couch and switched on his torch, he would be bound to see Jack.

The boy's heart pounded away, and his forehead felt suddenly wet. Kiki clung to his shoulder, feeling the fright of her master. She couldn't bear it any longer.

She suddenly rose into the air and flew at the head of the unseen man, giving one of the yelping screams she had picked up from the eagles. He uttered a startled exclamation, and tried to beat off the bird. His torch clattered to the floor. Jack hoped fervently that it was broken.

Kiki screeched again, this time like an express train, and the man lashed out at her. He caught a feather and ripped it out. Kiki found Jack once more, and perched on the crouching boy, growling like a dog.

'Good heavens, this place is full of birds and dogs!' said someone, in a disgusted voice, deep and hoarse. The man felt over the floor for his torch and at last found it.

'Broken!' he said and Jack heard the click as he tried to switch it on. 'One of those eagles, I suppose. What does it want to come indoors for?'

Muttering, the man went out. Jack heard a curious grating sound and then there was complete silence. He did not dare to get up for a long time, but crouched behind the enormous old sofa. Kiki appeared to have gone fast asleep on his shoulder.

At last he got cautiously up and tiptoed to the door, glad of his rubber shoes. He peeped out. There was now no light to be seen shining up dimly from underground. All was darkness and silence. Jack stared at the back of the hall. Somewhere over there had been a strange opening, leading to a hidden room – an old room, so full of strange things that it looked like a museum. Maybe it was the very room where the wicked old man had hidden his guests and starved them so that they were never heard of again! Jack didn't like the thought at all.

Without trying to see what had happened to the curious opening, he ran into the courtyard and made his way back to the old gorse bush. He felt safe there. He crawled in, accompanied by groans and protestations from Kiki, and tried to settle down to go to sleep again.

But he couldn't. His mind was full of that strange room, and he kept shuddering when he remembered how nearly he had been caught. If it hadn't been for old Kiki he would certainly have been discovered. Another step or two and the man, whoever he was, would almost have trodden on him!

He wished that the others were with him. He longed to tell them. Well, they would be up tomorrow, so he must wait in patience. There didn't seem any likelihood of the hidden man coming out in the daytime. He was keeping well hidden for some reason. He wouldn't expose his hiding place by day and come out.

'How does he get food?' Jack wondered. It was easy to get water from the pump. But what about food? Well, perhaps that was what he signalled about from the tower. His torch sent messages to friends. In that case other people might come. How in the world did they get in?

'I believe this is an adventure!' said Jack suddenly, and a funny feeling crept up his body. 'Yes, it is. It's the same feeling I had last year – when we sailed away to the Isle of Gloom, the Island of Adventure, where so many things happened to us. Golly, what will the others say when I tell them we've jumped straight into the middle of an adventure again! The Castle of Adventure! Philip was right when he called it that.'

After an hour or two of thinking and wondering, Jack at last fell asleep again. He awoke to find little fingers of sunlight coming through the gorse bush, and was glad that the day had come. He remembered the nighttime happenings, and wondered if that curious museum-like room could have been real.

'Well, I certainly couldn't have dreamt a room like that,' thought Jack, tickling Kiki to wake her. 'It would be impossible!'

He crawled out of the bush and breakfasted on biscuits and plums, which the others had brought to him the day before. He sat and looked thoughtfully at the castle. Who was hiding there?

Suddenly he went stiff and looked in amazement at two men walking through the courtyard. They were going towards the castle. How in the world had they got in? There simply *must* be some way in – or had the men keys to one of the big gates or doors?

The men went into the castle. Evidently unlike the hidden man, they did not fear being seen in daylight. 'Will the hidden man tell them he thought there was someone about last night?' thought Jack in a panic. 'Will they come and look for me?'

16

Things begin to happen

Jack crawled hurriedly back into the bush again, not waiting to wrap himself up in the rug, and getting terribly scratched. When he was inside he remembered that he had left some paper bags in the courtyard below, with some apple cores in them.

'Dash!' he thought. 'If those are found they'll know there's someone here besides themselves.'

He waited in the bush for an hour or so, taking peeps at

the eagles' nest now and again. He didn't know whether to hope the others would come soon, so that he would no longer be alone, or whether to hope that they would be late, to give the men a chance to go off again without seeing them.

'If they've chosen this for a safe hiding place for somebody, they won't be too pleased to know that we are here,' thought Jack uneasily. 'I suppose we really oughtn't to have come to the castle at all. I suppose it does belong to someone – those men perhaps!'

He heard the sound of voices and peeped between the prickly branches to see who it was. It was the two men again. The hidden man was evidently not going to risk coming out of his hiding place.

Jack peeped at them. They were great hulking men, one of them with a black beard. He didn't like their faces at all. As they came near he tried to hear what they said, but they were not talking any language he knew. That somehow made things all the stranger.

Suddenly they stopped, and with an exclamation the bearded man picked up Jack's paper bags. He saw the apple cores inside, and showed the other man. The cores were still moist, and Jack guessed that the men knew they had not been there very long! He squeezed himself hard into the hollow of the gorse bush, glad that it was so thick.

The men then separated and began to make a thorough search of the castle, the towers, the walls and the courtyard. Jack watched them through a chink in the bush. Kiki was absolutely quiet.

Then the men joined up and came across to the crag where the eagles nested. It was plain they were going to climb up to explore that place too, in case anyone was hiding there.

Jack crouched as still as a mouse when an owl is near. His heart began to beat painfully again. The men came right up the crag, and gave a cry of amazement when they saw the eagles' nest with the young one in.

Evidently they did not know the ways of eagles, for they went quite near to the nest and one of the men put out his hand.

There was a whirr of mighty wings and the female eagle seemed to drop like a stone from the sky on to the man's head. He turned away, whilst the other man beat off the angry bird. The attacked man put his arms across the top of his head to protect himself, and looked up at the male bird, scared, for that too was dropping quickly downwards.

Jack could see all this, and an idea came to him. He had a marvellous view of the first man the eagle had attacked – he was still looking up, showing the whole of his face, and his neck in an open-collared shirt. Jack pressed his camera release. Click! The man's photograph was taken, though unfortunately the other man was by then looking away, and his face was hidden.

Both men heard the click of the camera, and looked puzzled. Then, as the female eagle came at them again, they hurriedly descended the crag and ran down into the courtyard. They were not going to explore up there any more. In any case they both decided that nobody could possibly hide up there with fierce birds like that around!

Jack waited in the bush, watching the eagles, who had been much upset by the visit of the two men. Soon it was plain to Jack that they meant to take the young bird away from the nest. It must learn to fly! It could no longer be left in safety if two-legged creatures came right up to the nest.

The boy forgot his fears in his interest at the efforts of the two eagles to make the young one fly. They persuaded it to the edge of the nest, and then, with a push, dislodged it on to the ledge on which the nest was built. The young bird tried to get back again, but the female eagle flew round and round it, yelping, trying to tell it in all the eagle words she knew that it must go with her. The young one listened, or seemed to listen, then turned its head away, bored.

Then, for no reason that Jack could see, it suddenly spread out its wings. They were enormous. The boy had been taking snap after snap, and now he took a splendid picture of the young eagle trying out his wings.

The youngster flapped his wings so hard that he danced about on tiptoe – and then, most superbly, he took off from the ledge, and rose into the air, with his parents screaming on either side of him. He could fly!

'Marvellous!' said Jack, and cautiously took the roll of film from his camera. 'I wonder if they'll come back. It doesn't matter much if they don't, because I've got the most wonderful set of pictures now. Better than any anyone else has ever got!'

As he slipped a new roll of film into his camera, he heard the voices of the other children. He was very glad – but where were those men?

He crept out from the bush, hardly feeling the prickles, and climbed down to join them. They saw by his face that he had news for them. Lucy-Ann ran to him.

'Has anything happened, Jack? You look very serious! What do you think! We've come up with piles of things, because Mrs Mannering says we can stay for two or three days! She's got to go to Dinah's Aunt Polly, who has been taken ill again, but she'll be back soon.'

'And she thought we might as well join you up here if we wanted to!' said Dinah. 'But you don't look very thrilled about it, Jack!'

'Well, listen,' said Jack. 'There's something odd here. Really odd. I don't know if you ought to come. In fact, as I've really taken all the snaps I need to take of the eagles, I honestly think it would be better if we all went home.'

'Go back to Spring Cottage!' said Philip, in surprise. 'But why? Quick, tell us everything, Jack.'

'All right. But first, where's Tassie?' said Jack, looking round for the little gypsy girl.

'Her mother wouldn't let her come,' said Lucy-Ann. 'When Tassie told her we were all going to stay up at the castle with you, her mother nearly had a fit. She's like the villagers, you know – thinks there's something bad and creepy up here. She absolutely refused to let Tassie come. So we had to leave her behind.'

'She was in an awful temper with her mother,' said Philip; 'worse than any Dinah gets into. She flew at her mother and banged her hard. And her mother took hold of her and shook her like a rat. I think Tassie's got an awful mother. Anyway, she can't come. But go on – tell your story.'

'I suppose – I suppose you didn't by any chance meet anyone coming down the hill, did you?' said Jack suddenly, thinking that perhaps the two men had gone.

'We saw what looked like three men in the distance,' said Philip. 'Why?'

'What were they like? Did one have a black beard?' asked Jack.

'We couldn't possibly see what they were like, they were too far away, going down another path altogether,' said Philip. 'They might have been shepherds or anything. That's what *we* thought they were, anyway.'

'*Three* men,' said Jack thoughtfully. 'That looks as if the hidden man went too, then.'

'What *are* you talking about?' cried Dinah impatiently.

Jack began his story. The others listened in astonishment. When he described the hidden underground room, Lucy-Ann's eyes nearly fell out of her head!

'An underground room – with someone living there! Oh, I know what Tassie would say – she'd say it was that wicked old man still there!' cried Lucy-Ann. 'She'd say he would like to catch *us* and imprison us, so that no one ever heard of us again!'

'Don't be silly,' said Jack. 'The thing is – *something* is going on here, and we ought to find out what. I wish old Bill

Smuggs was here. He'd know what to do.'

'We don't even know his address,' said Philip. 'All we know is that he's in a town twenty miles away. And now Mother is away too, so we can't ask her advice either.'

'Well, whether she is away or not, I think we ought to go back to Spring Cottage,' said Jack soberly. 'We have dealt with dangerous men before, and it wasn't pleasant. I don't want to be mixed up in anything dangerous like that again. We'd better all go back.'

'Right,' said Philip. 'I agree with you. But, seeing that you think all three men are out of the way, what about having a squint at that hidden room? We might find something there to tell us who uses it and why.'

'All right,' said Jack. 'Come on. Kiki, come along too. Where's Button, Philip?'

'I left him with Tassie, to comfort her for not coming with us,' said Philip. 'She was so miserable. Anyway, she'll be pleased to see us back again so soon.'

They all went into the vast hall, and the boys switched on their torches. Sure that there was no one but themselves in the castle, they made no effort to be quiet, but talked and laughed in their usual way. Jack led them to the back of the hall, and looked at the floor.

There was no hole to be seen at all. It had gone completely. The children looked about for a trap-door in the floor, but there was none. Philip began to wonder if Jack had dreamt it all.

Then his sharp eyes saw a spike made of iron set deeply in the wall at the back of the hall. It shone as if it had been much handled. Philip took hold of it.

'Here's something strange!' he began, and pulled hard. The spike moved smoothly is some sort of groove, and suddenly there was a grating noise at Lucy-Ann's feet. She leapt back with a startled cry.

The ground was opening at her feet! A big stone there was

disappearing downwards in some mysterious fashion, and then swung itself smoothly to one side, exposing a short flight of stone steps, leading down into the hidden room that Jack had seen the night before. The children gasped.

'It reminds me of Ali Baba and the Forty Thieves or Aladdin and his cave!' said Dinah. 'Shall we go down? Do let's! This is most exciting.'

There was an oil lamp left burning on the long narrow table below, and by the light of this the children saw the room. Philip, Lucy-Ann and Dinah went eagerly down the steps to examine everything. They saw the tapestries on the walls, depicting old hunting scenes, they saw the old suits of armour standing round the room, and the big, heavy chairs that looked as if they were made for giants, not men.

'Where's Jack?' said Philip.

'Gone to get Kiki,' said Dinah. 'Oh, look, Philip, here's another spike in the wall, just like the one upstairs. What happens when you pull it?'

She pulled it – and with a grating noise the stone swung up and into place, imprisoning the three children down below!

17

Things go on happening

The three children watched the great stone slide into place like magic. It was an extraordinary sight. But Philip suddenly felt worried.

'Dinah! Let me have that spike. Move away. I hope to goodness it will move the stone back again!'

The boy pulled at it, but it remained fixed. He tried to move it the other way. He jerked it. It would not move at all.

'It closes the hole in the floor, but it doesn't open it,' he said. He looked round for another spike or lever or handle – anything that he thought might open the hole to allow them to get out – but he could see nothing.

'There must be *some*thing!' he said, 'or the man that hides here wouldn't be able to come out at night. There must be *some*thing!'

The two girls were scared. They didn't like being shut up like this in an underground room. Lucy-Ann felt as if all the suits of armour were watching her and enjoying her fright. She didn't like them.

'Well, Philip, Jack will be along soon,' said Dinah, 'and he'll see the hole is shut and will work the spike upstairs in the hall to open it again. We needn't worry.'

'I suppose he will,' said Philip, looking relieved. 'You are an idiot, Dinah, messing about with things before you know what they do.'

'Well, you'd have done the same thing yourself,' retorted Dinah.

'All right, all right,' said Philip. He began to look all round the peculiar room. The suits of armour interested him. He wished he could put one on, just for fun!

An idea came to him. 'I say, I'll play a trick on Jack!' he said. 'I'll get inside one of these suits of armour, and hide. Then when Jack opens the hole and comes down don't you tell him where I am – and I'll suddenly step off one of these pedestals the armour is on, with a frightful clanging noise and scare him stiff!'

The girls laughed. 'All right,' said Lucy-Ann. 'Hurry up. Do you know how to get into one?'

'Yes. I've tried one before, when we had one at school to examine,' said Philip. 'It's quite easy when you know how. You can help me.'

Before long Philip was in the suit of armour. He had the helmet on his head, and the visor over his face. He could see quite well through the visor, but nobody would know there was anyone inside the armoured suit! He got back on the pedestal with a lot of clanking. The girls giggled.

'Won't Jack get an awful shock! I wish he'd come,' said Lucy-Ann.

'Are you comfortable, Philip?' asked Dinah, looking at her armoured brother standing quite still on his wooden pedestal, looking for all the world exactly like the others around.

'Fairly,' said Philip. 'But golly, I wouldn't much like to go to war in this – I'd never be able to walk more than a few yards! How they fought in them, those old-time soldiers, I really don't know!'

The girls wandered round the room. They looked at the tapestry scenes. They sat in the enormous old chairs. They fingered the ancient weapons that were arranged here and there. It certainly was a curious room.

'What *is* Jack doing?' said Lucy-Ann, at last, beginning to feel anxious. 'He's been simply ages. Oh, Dinah – you don't think those men have come back, do you – and captured him?'

'I shouldn't think so,' said Dinah, also beginning to feel worried. 'I can't imagine what he's doing. After all, he'd only got to call Kiki, wait for her to come to him and then follow us!'

'You know,' said a hollow voice from inside the suit of armour, 'you know, I don't believe those men we saw *were* the men from the castle. I've suddenly thought – they couldn't be!'

'What do you mean?' cried both girls, staring in dismay at the place where Philip's face was behind the visor.

'Well, think where we saw them,' said Philip. 'We saw them a good way down the hill, just above the farm, didn't we? We know there's no path up to the castle there. And now I think the matter over carefully, I'm pretty certain they were men belonging to the farm. One was that enormously tall fellow we sometimes see when we fetch eggs.'

The girls thought hard. Yes, that was where the men had been seen – just above the old farm.

'I believe you're right, Philip,' said Lucy-Ann, scared. 'And anyway, if they didn't want to be seen, it would be silly to take the farm path, wouldn't it? All the farm dogs would bark at them, and the farmer would look out.'

'Yes – and the dogs were *not* barking, or we would have heard them,' said Philip. 'So that rather proves our point. Dash! I don't believe those were Jack's men, after all. It's quite likely they never left the castle, and are still somewhere about.'

'I do wonder what Jack is doing,' said Dinah. 'I do wish he'd come.'

Jack was certainly a long time coming – but he couldn't help it! He had gone after Kiki, who had flown into the furnished room in which they had both hidden the night before – and suddenly, from the window, he had seen the three men in a corner of the yard!

'Golly!' thought the boy, 'Philip was wrong – the men he saw weren't the ones from the castle! They must have been farm workers seeing to the sheep or something. My word, I hope they're not going to that hidden room!'

The boy darted back into the hall, and went to the place where the hole should be. But it was gone, and a stone now covered the entrance to the room. He was surprised. He had no idea, of course, that Dinah had found the lever below and used it, closing the entrance.

He debated what to do. Should he open the hole and see if the others were down there? Would the men come into the hall just as he was doing it? He could hear their voices quite clearly now.

Jack darted back into the furnished room and, accidentally touching a chair as he went, raised a cloud of dust at once. He ran to the wide window and hid behind a long tapestry curtain there. He did not dare to touch it, because he felt sure it would fall to pieces in his hands.

The men were evidently still worried about the bag of apple cores. It was obvious that they knew someone was there besides themselves – and then, to Jack's dismay, he saw that they had found the pile of things the others had brought up with them that morning!

They had brought them from the courtyard and had spread them out at the entrance to the castle, looking through them carefully. Jack caught one or two words, but he couldn't understand them.

'We shall have to get out of here the very first moment possible,' thought the boy. 'We may get into serious trouble. If only I could get everyone up into the room with the plank!'

Two of the men now separated and went off into the castle, evidently to make another good search. The third man stood at the great doorway, puffing at a cigarette and apparently keeping a watch over the courtyard.

It was impossible for Jack to open the way to the hidden room, for the man at the doorway would see and hear him. There was nothing to do but wait, and hope for a chance to do it before any of the men did it themselves.

So the boy stood behind the curtain, watching and waiting. He wished Bill Smugs was there! Bill always knew what to do when things were awkward – but then Bill was a grown-up and grown-ups knew how to handle things in the right way, somehow.

The man at the doorway finished his cigarette. He did not throw the end away but carefully stubbed it out against a coin he took from his pocket, and put it into a little tin box. Evidently he was not going to leave any signs about that would tell anyone he was living there.

He turned and came into the hall. Jack heard his feet

echoing, and held his breath. Was he going back to the hidden room?

He was! He walked to the back of the hall, and felt about in the wall there for the spike. Jack, fearing that he was doing this, crept to the door of the room he was hiding in, and peered through the crack. From there he could see what happened.

The man pulled at the spike, and the stone moved with a grating sound, first downwards and then to the side. It was a marvellous piece of mechanism, very old, but still in perfect working order.

Jack's heart almost stood still. Now what was going to happen? What would the man say when he saw the other three?

Dinah and Lucy-Ann heard the grating noise of the stone as it moved, and looked up. Philip peered through his visor, hoping Jack was coming at last. But to their horror a man stood on the steps, looking at them in the greatest astonishment and anger!

He could only see Dinah and Lucy-Ann, of course. The two girls stared at him and trembled. His face was not a pleasant one. He had an enormous nose, narrow eyes, and the thinnest lips imaginable. Shaggy eyebrows hung over his eyes, almost like a sheepdog's hair.

'So!' said the man, and narrowed his eyes still more. 'So! You come here, and you go to my room. What is the meaning of this?'

The girls were terrified, and Lucy-Ann began to sob. Jack, listening, longed to push the man down the steps and break his neck! 'Hateful fellow, frightening poor Lucy-Ann like that!' thought the boy angrily, wishing he dared to show himself and comfort her.

Then he heard the footsteps of the other two men returning from their hunt. The first man heard them too and went back up the stairs to the top. He called to the others in a language Jack did not understand, evidently telling them to come and see what he had found.

Philip, still hidden in the suit of armour, took the opportunity of whispering instructions to the girls. 'Don't be frightened. They'll probably only think you're two girls visiting the old castle. You tell them that. Don't say a word about me or Jack, or we shan't be able to help you. Jack's up there somewhere, we know, and he'll look out for you and get you away. I'll stay down here till I can escape myself. They won't know I'm in the armour.'

He couldn't say any more, because all three men now came down the steps and into the hidden room. One man had a dense black beard, the other was clean-shaven, but the man the girls had already seen was the ugliest of a really ugly trio.

Lucy-Ann began to cry again. Dinah was very scared, but she would not cry.

'What are you here for?' asked the shaggy-browed man. 'Now – you tell us everything – or you may be very very sorry!'

18

Prisoners in the castle

'We only came to have a look at the castle,' said Dinah, trying to keep her voice from trembling. 'Does it belong to you? We didn't know.'

'How did you find this room?' demanded the bearded man, scowling.

'By accident,' said Dinah. 'We were so surprised. Please let us go. We're only two girls, and we didn't mean any harm.'

'Does anyone outside this castle know we are here, or anything about this room?' asked the shaggy man.

'No, nobody,' said Dinah truthfully. 'We have never seen you before this moment, and we only found the room today. Please, do let us go!'

'I suppose you've been messing about here for some days,' said the man. 'We found your things. Interfering little trespassers!'

'We didn't know the castle belonged to anyone,' said Dinah, again. 'How could we know? No one ever comes here. The villagers keep away from the place.'

'Is anyone with you?' asked the bearded man, suspiciously.

'Well, you can see that for yourselves,' said Dinah, hoping fervently that none of the men would think of looking into the suits of armour standing round the room.

'We've looked all over the place,' said the third man to the shaggy one. 'There's no one else here, that we do know!'

'Please let us go,' begged Dinah. 'We won't come here again, we promise.'

'Ah – but you will go home and you will tell about things you have found here and seen here, isn't that so?' said the bearded man, in a horrid, smooth kind of voice. 'No, little missies – you must stay here till our work is done. Then, when it no longer matters, maybe we shall let you go. I said *maybe*! It depends on how you behave.'

Philip trembled with anger inside the suit of armour. How dared these men speak like that to the two girls? But the boy did not dare to show himself. That might only make things worse.

'Well,' said the bearded man, 'We have business to discuss. You may leave this room, but do not go beyond our call.'

To the girls' intense relief the men allowed them to go up the stone steps into the hall. Then the hole closed once more, and they were left alone.

'We must escape,' whispered Dinah, taking Lucy-Ann's hand. 'We must get away immediately and bring help to Philip. I daren't think what would happen to him if those men found him.'

'Where's Jack?' sobbed Lucy-Ann. 'I want him.'

Jack was not far away. As soon as he heard the stone close the hole up, and recognised the girls' voices, he darted out of the old drawing room. Lucy-Ann saw him and ran to him gladly.

He put his arms round her, and patted her. 'It's all right, Lucy-Ann, it's all right. We'll soon be out of here, and we'll get help to rescue Philip. Don't worry. Don't cry any more.'

But Lucy-Ann couldn't stop crying, though now she cried more from relief at having Jack again than from fright. The boy guided her to the wide stone stairs that led to the upper rooms of the castle.

'We'll get across the plank in no time,' he said. 'Then we'll be safe. We'll soon rescue Philip too. Don't be afraid.'

Up they went and up, then along the long corridor, lit dimly by its slit windows. They came to the room they used for the plank.

Dinah ran gladly to the window, eager to slip across to safety. But she paused in dismay. There was no plank.

'We're in the wrong room!' she said. 'Oh, quick, Jack, find the right one!'

They ran out and into the next room – but there was no plank on the sill there either. Then into the next room further on they went – but again there was no plank.

'This is like a bad dream,' said Dinah, trembling. 'We shall go into room after room, and the plank will never be there! Oh, Jack – is this a nightmare?'

'It seems like one,' said the boy. 'Come now – we're upset and excited – we'll begin at the bottom of the corridor and work our way along each room – then we shall find the right one.'

But they didn't. Room after room had no welcome plank on its sill. At the last room the children paused.

'I'm afraid,' said Jack, 'I'm very much afraid that the men discovered how we got in – and removed the plank!'

'Oh dear!' said Dinah, and sat down suddenly on the dusty floor. 'My legs won't hold me up any more. I suppose the men would never have let Lucy-Ann and me out of the hidden room unless they had discovered our way in, and made it impossible for us to escape that way.'

'Yes – if we'd stopped to think for a moment we'd have guessed that ourselves,' said Jack, gloomily. He also sat down on the floor to consider things. 'I wonder where they put the plank. It might be a good idea to look for it.'

'They've probably just tipped it off the sill and left it lying on the ground,' said Dinah, just as gloomily.

'No, they wouldn't do that, in case anyone else *did* happen to know that way in,' said Jack. 'We'd better look for it.'

So they hunted all over the place, but there was no sign of the plank at all. Wherever it was, it was too well hidden for the children to find. They gave it up after a bit.

'Well, what are we going to do, now that we can't escape?' said Dinah. 'Do stop sniffing, Lucy-Ann. It doesn't do any good.'

'Don't bother her,' said Jack, who felt sorry for his small sister. 'This is pretty serious. Here we are, stuck in this old castle with no way of escape – and Philip down below in the hidden room in great danger of being discovered. He's only got to sneeze or cough, you know!'

Lucy-Ann pondered this statement of alarm. She at once imagined poor Philip trying to stifle sneeze after sneeze.

'We've apparently fallen headlong into some strange mystery,' said Jack. 'I can't make head or tail of it. Why these men want to hide up here, I don't know. But they are ugly customers – nasty fellows, each one of them. They must belong to a gang of some sort, up to some mischief. I'd like to put a stop to it, but it's impossible as things are. The only good things about the whole affair are that the men don't know *I'm* here, and they don't know that Philip is hidden in their secret meeting place!'

'If only we could get out!' sighed Lucy-Ann. 'I know Aunt Allie is away, but we could get hold of the farmer or someone.'

'I don't see how we can possibly get out, now that our one and only way of getting in is gone,' said Jack. 'I don't think even Tassie will come up, now that her mother has threatened her with a hiding if she does.'

'We mustn't let the men know you're here too, Jack,' said Dinah. 'Where will you hide for safety?'

'In the middle of my gorsebush,' said Jack. 'That's as safe as anywhere. You girls go down to the hall and see if that room is still shut – if it is I'll slip down and go up the crag to my gorse bush. You can sit about the rocks there and whisper to me what goes on.'

'I wish we knew where Button got in and out,' said Lucy-Ann. 'If we did we might try his way. Only I suppose if it's a rabbit hole it would be far too narrow for us.'

They made their way to the hall. The stone was still in place over the hidden room. They beckoned Jack down, and he sped across the hall, out of the great doorway, across the courtyard and up the craggy, gorse-grown rock in the corner to the safety of his hiding place. He crawled in, and the bush closed round him.

The girls climbed up the rocks to be near him. From there they had a good view of everything to do with the castle. They undid a packet of food and began to have a meal, though Lucy-Ann choked over almost every mouthful. They handed Jack some food through the prickly branches of the bush.

'Good thing we brought up such stacks of food,' said Dinah. 'If we are going to be prisoners for ages it's just as well!'

'Of course, if your mother hadn't gone away she would have got worried when we didn't go home, and have sent a search party up to the castle,' said Lucy-Ann. 'It's bad luck she should have gone away just now! No one will miss us at all.'

'Sh! Here are two of the men!' said Dinah. 'Don't say a word more, Jack.'

The men gave a loud shout for the two girls. Dinah answered sulkily. They beckoned to them to come down from the crag.

'And did you find your little plank?' enquired the bearded man politely, and the other man sniggered.

'No. You took it away,' said Dinah sullenly.

'Of course. It was such a good idea of yours – but we didn't like it,' said the man. 'Now, you cannot get away, you know that. So you may stay here unharmed in the court-yard, and at night you may sleep peacefully in the big bed downstairs, for we have work to do that will take us else-where. But we forbid you to go up to the towers, or upstairs at all. We are not going to have you signalling for help. You understand that if you disobey us, you will be very sorry – and you will probably be put down into a dungeon we know of, where rats and mice and beetles live.'

Dinah shuddered. The very idea filled her with horror.

'So you be good girls and obedient, and no harm will come to you,' said the bearded man. 'Always be where we can see you, somewhere in this courtyard, and come when we call. You have plenty of food, we know. And there is water in the kitchen, if you pump it.'

The girls did not answer. The men walked off and dis-appeared once more into the castle.

'What's happening to Philip?' said Lucy-Ann, after a pause. 'Will he starve down there? I wish we could rescue him.'

'He won't starve. There's plenty of food on the table, if only he can step off his pedestal and get it,' said Dinah. 'If only we could send word to Tassie! She might get help. But there is no way of sending word.'

'I suppose Kiki wouldn't go, with a note tied to her leg, like pigeons have in wartime?' said Lucy-Ann. 'No, I'm sure she wouldn't leave Jack. She's an awfully clever and sensible bird, but it would be too much to expect her to become a messenger for us.'

However, a messenger did turn up – a most unexpecred one, but a very welcome one indeed!

19

Lucy-Ann has an idea

All that day the girls hung about the courtyard, never keeping very far from the crag, so that they could talk co poor bored Jack in his hiding place. They wondered how Philip was getting on down in the hidden room. Had he been discovered?

'It's a great pıty those men talk together in some language we don't understand,' said Dinah. 'If they talked in English Philip might learn quite a lot of secrets, standing there so close beside them, without them knowing!'

'Yes, he might,' said Lucy-Ann. 'I wish he wasn't down there though. I should feel so scared if it was me, hidden ın armour that might creak or clank if I moved just a little bit.'

'Well, Philip won't feel scared,' said Dinah, 'He is hardly ever scared of anything. I expect he is quite enioying himself.'

But Lucy-Ann didn't believe that for one moment. She thought Dinah was silly to say such a thing. But then, Dinah wasn't as fond of her brother as she, Lucy-Ann, was. It was bad enough to have Jack being compelled to hide in that horrid gorse bush – but it would have been far worse to have him down in the hidden room with the men, likely to be discovered at any moment!

'Cheer up!' whispered Jack, from the gorse bush, seeing her gloomy face. 'This is an adventure, you know.'

'I only like adventures afterwards,' said Lucy-Ann. 'I don't like them when they're happening. I didn't want this adventure at all. We didn't look for it, we just seemed to fall into the middle of it!'

'Well, never mind. It'll turn out all right, I expect,' said Jack comfortingly.

But poor Lucy-Ann couldn't see how. It was quite clear that they couldn't escape from the castle, and equally clear that no one could rescue them.

They had tea on the crag, the girls passing food to Jack, who was now feeling very cramped indeed, and longed to get out and stretch his legs. But he didn't dare to. When night came he would, but not till then.

The sun went down. Kiki, bored with her long imprisonment, became very talkative. The girls let her talk, keeping a sharp look-out in case the men came and heard her.

'Poor old Kiki, what a pity, what a pity! Put the kettle on, God save the Queen! Now, now, now, now, attention please! Sit up straight and don't loll. How many times have I told you to pop the weasel?'

The girls giggled. Kiki was very funny when she talked, for she brought into her chattering all the words and sentences she knew, running them one into another in a most bewildering way.

'Good old Kiki!' said Jack, scratching her neck. 'You're bored, aren't you? Never mind, you shall have a fine fly round when it's dark. Now don't start your express engine screech, or you'll bring our enemies up here at a run!'

The sun sank lower. Long shadows lay across the courtyard and then the whole of it went into twilight. The stars came out one by one, pricking the sky here and there.

The men came up the yard, two of them together. They called the girls.

'Hey, you two girls! You'd better come down and go to bed.'

'We don't mind the dark. We'll stay a bit longer,' shouted back Dinah, who wanted to walk round the yard with Jack, before she and Lucy-Ann retired to the hidden room.

'Well, come down in half an hour,' shouted the bearded man. 'It will be quite dark then, and you'd be better inside.'

They disappeared. Dinah slipped down from her perch and went silently after them. She saw them going down the steps of the hidden room. Then she heard the now familiar grating noise as the entrance hole was closed by the sliding stone.

She ran back to Jack. 'Come on, Jack,' she whispered. 'The men are down in the hidden room, and it's almost dark now. You'll be safe if you come out.'

Very glad to come from his uncomfortable hiding-place, Jack squeezed out of the bush. He stood up thankfully and stretched his arms high above his head.

'Golly, I'm stiff!' he said. 'Come on, let's go for a nice sharp walk round the courtyard. It's too dark for me to be seen now.'

They set off, linking their arms together. They hadn't gone more than halfway before something hurled itself against them out of the shadows, and almost knocked Jack over. He stopped, startled.

'What's that? Where's my torch?'

He flicked it on quickly, and then off again, in case the men were about. He gave a low cry.

'It's Button! Dear little old Button – *how* did you get here?

I *am* glad to see you!'

Button made happy noises in his throat, rolled over like a puppy, licked the girls and Jack, and generally behaved as if he was mad with delight. But he kept going off to the side and back again, and it was soon clear to the others that he had come to find Philip, his master.

'You can't get to Philip, old boy,' said Jack, fondling the little fox cub. 'You'll have to make do with us. Philip isn't here.'

The fox cub made a barking noise, and Kiki, who was sitting on Jack's shoulder, evidently rather disgusted to see Button appear again, immediately imitated the barking. Button jumped up, trying to reach her, but he couldn't. Kiki made a jeering noise, which would have been most infuriating to Button if he had understood it, but he didn't.

'Jack! I've got an idea!' said Lucy-Ann, suddenly clutching her brother's arm.

'What!' said Jack, who never thought very much of Lucy-Ann's good ideas.

'Can't we use Button as a messenger? Can't we send him back to Tassie with a note, telling her to get help for us, Jack? Button is sure to go back to her when he can't find Philip, because, next to Philip, he loves Tassie. Can't we do that?'

'Jack! That's really a good idea of Lucy-Ann's!' said Dinah, in excitement. 'Button is the only one of us who knows how to get out of here. He could be our messenger, as Lucy-Ann says.'

Jack considered it. 'Well,' he said, 'I must say it seems a sound idea, and worth trying. It can't do any harm, anyway. All right, we'll make Button our messenger.'

The next thing was to write a note to Tassie. Jack had a notebook, and he tore out a page. He wrote a few words in pencil and read them out to the others.

'Tassie, we are imprisoned here. Get help as soon as you

can. We may be in serious danger.'

They all signed it. Then Jack folded it up and wondered how to get Button to take it.

He thought of a way at last. He had some string in his pocket, and first of all he tied the note tightly round and round with it. Then he twisted the string fairly tightly round Button's sturdy little neck. He knew that if he made it too loose the fox cub would work it off over his head, for, like all wild things, he resented anything tied to him.

'There,' said Jack, pleased. 'I don't think Button can get that off, and the note is tied very tightly to the string. I've made him a kind of string collar, with the note at the front, under his chin.'

'Go back to Tassie, Button,' said Lucy-Ann. But Button didn't understand. He still hoped Philip would appear, and he didn't want to go back until he had seen him – or, better still, he would stay with him if he could. So the little fox cub hunted all around for Philip again and again, occasionally stopping and trying to get off this new thing round his neck. But he couldn't.

Suddenly one of the men called loudly, making everyone jump violently. 'Come in, you two girls!'

'Good night, Jack. We must go,' whispered Lucy-Ann, giving her brother a hug. 'I hope you won't be too uncomfortable tonight. Take some of our extra rugs into the bush with you, when you go to sleep.'

'I shan't go back to that beastly bush for ages,' said Jack, who was thoroughly tired of his hiding place and would have been glad never to see it again. 'Good night. Don't worry about anything. Once Button gets to Tassie, she'll soon bring help.'

The girls left him in the dark courtyard. They went into the hall, and saw the dim light of the lamp shining up from the hidden room. They went down the stone steps, and looked hurriedly round. Was Philip still in the suit of armour? They couldn't tell. All the suits of armour were standing around as usual, but whether one had Philip inside or not they didn't know.

'We're going to shut you in here,' said the shaggy man, his ugly face looking even uglier in the lamplight. 'You can use that bed to sleep in. We shall see you in the morning.'

He went up the steps, and then the stone swung sideways and upwards, closing the hole completely. The girls were prisoners once again. They stood in silence for a moment or two listening. There was nothing to be heard.

'Philip!' whispered Lucy-Ann, looking at the suit of armour in which she had last seen him. 'Are you there? Speak to us!'

'I'm still here,' came Philip's voice, sounding queerly hollow. 'But I hope I never have to spend another day like this. I'm going to get out of this armour. I can't stay in it another minute!'

'Oh, Philip – do you think you'd better?' said Dinah anxiously. 'Suppose the men come back?'

'I don't think they will – but if they do I jolly well can't help it. I'm desperate,' said Philip. 'I've got cramp in all my limbs, I'm tired out with standing so still and I've had to stop myself sneezing at least three times. It's been a most awful strain, I can tell you.'

A clanking noise came from the suit of armour as Philip began to get out of it, clumsily and awkwardly, for he felt very stiff.

'The worst of it was my toad couldn't bear being in here with me and he got out through a crack, and hopped and crawled about for all he was worth,' said Philip. 'The men saw him and were awfully surprised.'

Dinah looked about at once for the toad. She hoped it wasn't anywhere near her.

'Poor old Philip,' said Lucy-Ann, going to help. 'You must have had an awful day.'

'I have – but I wouldn't really have missed it for worlds!' said Philip. 'My word, I've learnt a few things, I can tell you! For instance, there's a secret way out of this room – behind the tapestry somewhere!'

'Oooh,' said Lucy-Ann, looking at the tapestry, as if she expected to see a secret way opening before her eyes. 'Is there really? How do you know?'

'I'll tell you all about it, once I get out of this awful armour,' said Philip. 'My word, I hope I never wear it again! You wouldn't believe how hot I got inside it. There – I'm out, thank goodness! Now to stretch myself a bit!'

'And then tell us what happened in here today,' said Dinah, eager to hear. 'I bet you've got some exciting things to tell us!'

She was right. Philip certainly had!

20

Philip tells a strange story

'We'd better get on the bed, in case those awful men come back,' said Dinah. 'What will you do if they do, Philip?'

'I shall hear the grating noise the stone makes when it moves, and I'll hop out of the bed and get underneath it,' said Philip. 'I don't really think the men will suspect there is anyone here but you – they're not likely suddenly to make a search in the middle of the night!'

There was plenty of room for them all on the enormous old bed. There was an eiderdown mattress, which the three children sank into. Philip was pleased. After the hardness of the suit of armour, it was pleasant to feel something so soft.

He sat up and told his story.

'Well, you remember when you went up the steps by

yourselves and left me there?' he said. 'I was awfully angry to think those men should talk to you like that, but I couldn't do anything about it, of course. Anyway, I just stayed put for ages, and after some time all three men came down, shut up the entrance hole, and sat round the table.'

'Could you understand their talk?' asked Lucy-Ann.

'No, more's the pity, I couldn't,' said Philip. 'They had maps out, and were tracing things on them, but I couldn't see what. I almost over-balanced myself, trying to see.'

'Gracious! What a shock you'd have given those men if you had toppled over with a crash,' said Dinah, with a laugh. 'Good thing you didn't though.'

'Well, they sat about for a long time, talking and poring over their maps,' said Philip, 'and then they had a jolly good meal. They opened stacks of tins. It made my mouth water to see them.'

'Poor Philip – have you had anything to eat?' asked Lucy-Ann.

Philip nodded. 'Don't worry. The very next time the men disappeared up the stone steps and shut the hole, I clanked off my pedestal, and finished up most of what they had left. I had to hope they wouldn't notice it was gone. But I was so hungry and thirsty I didn't care. It was funny to see all the other suits of armour standing round, looking at me. I half expected them to walk up and join me in my meal!'

'Don't say things like that!' said poor Lucy-Ann, looking quite scared. She gazed with wide eyes at the suits of armour standing so silently on their pedestals, and imagined them suddenly walking off them, with a clash and a clank.

Philip laughed, and gave Lucy-Ann a pat. 'It was awfully difficult to drink,' he said. 'I couldn't tip my head back properly in that armour. I poured half of it down the inside of it, and I was terrified I'd have puddles coming out of my feet, when I went back.'

The girls couldn't help laughing. Philip always told a

story very well, making them see every detail of it.

'Well, I got back to my pedestal, feeling a whole lot better, and hadn't been there more than twenty minutes or so when the men came back again. And then an extraordinary thing happened.'

'What?' said the girls together, holding their breath.

'See the tapestry over there – the one with the dogs and the horses on?' said Philip, pointing. 'Exactly opposite where my suit of armour stands? Well, behind there is a secret door!'

He paused and the girls gazed first at the tapestry and then at Philip. 'The men talked a bit, and then one of them went to that piece of tapestry. He lifted it up and hung it back on that nail you can see. I could see everything perfectly through my visor. Well, at first I couldn't make out what the man was doing, because the wall looked as if it was made of solid stone all along.'

'And wasn't it?' said Lucy-Ann, in excitement.

'No,' said Philip. 'Part of it is only a thin slab of stone, not immensely solid and thick like the rest of the walls here, and that thin piece slides right back! Then when it had moved back, the man stepped into the square hollow place left and felt about there. On one side of the hollow place was a door of some kind, which he opened – and all three men disappeared through the door!'

'Gracious!' said Dinah. 'Where did they go?'

'I don't know,' said Philip. 'But I'd dearly like to! There's some secret here, some big mystery. Those men are up to some mischief. Why should foreigners – because two of them *are* foreigners, you can tell that by their accent – why should foreigners come to a lonely place like this, and hide and have meetings, and use secret rooms and doors?'

'Shall we see where that door leads to?' said Dinah, overcome with curiosity.

'No, don't let's,' said Lucy-Ann, who had had enough excitement for one day.

'You're scared,' said Dinah scornfully.

'No, she's not, said Philip. 'Anyway, I think it would be a mistake to mess about behind that tapestry just now. If the men happened to come back and saw that we had found their secret door, goodness knows what they'd do. We might never be heard of again!'

Dinah was silent. She longed to explore behind that tapestry – but she knew Philip was right. They must wait and take their time. Dinah began to tell Philip about their day with Jack in the courtyard, and all that had happened. He was very glad that Jack hadn't been caught.

'Well, that's two people those men have no idea are here,' he said. 'Me and Jack. That's good. As long as they think it's only a couple of girls they've got to deal with, they won't be so much on their guard.'

Then Dinah told him about sending Button with a message to Tassie. He listened thoughtfully, and then made a remark that sent their hearts down into their boots.

'It was fine idea,' he said, 'but it won't be a bit of good, I'm afraid. You've forgotten that Tassie can't read or write!'

The two girls stared at one another in the greatest dismay. They *had* forgotten that. Of course – Tassie wouldn't be able to make head or tail of the note. What a blow! Lucy-Ann looked very woebegone to think that her good idea shouldn't have been so very good after all.

Philip put his arm round her and gave her a friendly hug. 'Never mind. Perhaps Tassie will have the common sense to show the note to somebody who *can* read! Cheer up.'

This exchange of news took a long time. The girls began to feel sleepy. Lucy-Ann lay down on the soft bed and shut her eyes. Dinah and Philip talked a little longer and then lay down too. Philip was tired with his long day in the suit of armour, and fell sound asleep almost at once.

Dinah was awakened suddenly, two or three hours later, by the sound of the entrance hole being opened. At first she did not recognise the noise – then, very suddenly, she knew what it was. In a rush it all came back to her.

Philip and Lucy-Ann did not awake. Dinah shook the boy desperately. 'Philip!' she whispered urgently. 'Wake up! Quick, get under the bed! They're here!'

Half asleep, Philip rolled off the bed, and underneath it, just as the first man came down the steps. Dinah lay still as if she was asleep. Lucy-Ann did not stir.

The man, hearing the noise of Philip falling off the bed, stared suspiciously over into the corner where the four-poster bed stood. He turned up the wick of the oil lamp, which had burned down, and went over to the bed.

His toe almost touched Philip who was crouching underneath. The man pulled back the heavy curtains around the old bed and looked down at the girls. Dinah felt sure he knew she was awake.

He stared down at the two of them for a few seconds and then pulled the curtains back again. Apparently he was satisfied that the girls were really asleep. He did not dream that a third child was there, hidden safely under the bed!

Dinah, looking between her eyelashes, saw that there were five men there, two that she had not seen before. They spoke in a language she could not understand. One of the men she knew unlocked a big drawer in a chest, and took out a roll of maps, which he threw on the table.

Then, one after another, the maps were spread out and apparently discussed. Finally they were put back again, and the drawer locked. Then, to Dinah's excited delight, the shaggy-brown man threw back a piece of tapestry from the wall, and exposed the place where the secret door was hidden.

One of the men laid his hand on his arm, saying something in a low voice, and nodding towards the bed in the further corner.

Then he walked swiftly across the bed and drew the thick

curtains so closely round it that Dinah could see nothing more. How annoying! She did not dare to peep, because she knew if she did, she would probably be seen.

After that she could only lie and listen, wondering what was happening. She heard a sliding noise, a click, a little thud, and the sound of a key turning in a lock. Then she heard voices again. After that she heard men going up the stone stair, and peeped quickly to see who they were. They were the three she knew. Evidently the others had gone through the secret door, to wherever that led to. It was all most mysterious.

There came the familiar grating noise – and then silence. Dinah peeped out. There was no one in the room. The tapestry was replaced, and hung down over the wall again.

She called softly to Philip, and he came out from under the bed. 'Don't wake Lucy-Ann, or she won't go to sleep again,' said Philip in a low voice. 'Did you see much, Dinah?'

'Lots,' said Dinah, and told him everything. Philip listened intently.

'Five men now,' he said. 'I do wonder what they're all up to. You see, Dinah, it was much the best thing not to go messing about trying to find that secret door tonight. We'd have been properly caught if we had!'

'Yes, we should,' said Dinah. 'Philip, what *are* these men up to?'

'I don't know,' said Philip. 'If we went through that hidden door, and found out where it led to, we might learn their secret. But we must wait and take our chance, not just rush in without thinking.'

'I shouldn't think they'll come back again, would you?' said Dinah, lying down. 'Do you think you'd better sleep under the bed, in case? You made an awful noise rolling off.'

'Perhaps I'd better,' said Philip. He took one of the blankets off the bed and went underneath it, arranging himself as comfortably as he could.

'Are you going to stand in that suit of armour again tomorrow?' asked Dinah suddenly.

'No, rather not! I'll hide under the bed. I'm sure the men won't dream of looking for someone they don't know is there!' said Philip. 'I feel as if I never want to see a suit of armour again in my life! Beastly, uncomfortable things!'

They fell asleep again, and this time nothing disturbed them till the morning. It was impossible to tell whether it was morning or not in the hidden room, but Dinah's watch showed her that it was half-past seven.

The shaggy man came down into the room. 'You can clear out for the day,' he said. 'But keep within sight and call as I told you – or most unpleasant things might happen!'

21

Another day goes by

Jack felt lonely when the girls had gone down the steps to the hidden room for the night. He was left up in the courtyard with Kiki, and he felt bored.

'I hope the girls will be all right,' he thought. 'Oh, hallo, Button, are you still here? Why don't you go back to Tassie? You won't be able to get to Philip, you know.'

The fox cub whined and rubbed his head against Jack, asking him as plainly as a fox cub could to take him to his beloved Philip.

'Listen. You go back to Tassie with that note,' said Jack, still forgetting that Tassie couldn't read a word. 'Go on, Button. Once you get to Tassie, things will be easier for us, because when she reads that note, she will get help.'

Button stayed in the courtyard with Jack almost all night long. He didn't give up hope of finding Philip, and kept going off to hunt for him. Kiki was very scornful of him but Button took no notice of her.

The moon came up and lighted the courtyard strangely. An owl hooted, and Kiki at once mimicked it perfectly. The owl came into the yard on silent wings, to look for the one who had answered. Kiki was delighted. She kept hooting softly from one place and another, and the owl was astonished to find what seemed to him to be a perfect host of owls all over the place, calling first from one spot and then another.

Jack enjoyed the fun. Then suddenly he saw the three men standing in the moonlight, and felt glad that he had not been wandering about, for he would certainly have been seen.

He slipped away into the shadows of the great wall, and came near to the enormous door that stood facing what had once been the road to the castle. He sat down by a big bush, knowing it would hide him completely.

Suddenly he jumped violently, and stared as if he could not believe his eyes. The big door was opening! It swung slowly back without a sound, and where it had been was now a moonlit space, gateway to the outer world!

Jack half rose – but sank back again. Two men entered the castle yard, and then the great solid door closed silently behind them. There was a loud click, and then the two men passed quite close to Jack. They did not see him, for he was in black shadow. He crouched down like a toad against the earth.

The men passed and soon joined the other two. Then they all disappeared into the castle. Jack imagined they were going down to the hidden room – as indeed they were.

He waited till they had gone, and then made his way as quickly as he could to the big door in the high wall. If only he could open it! If only he could get out, and go down the hillside, even if he had to walk over the treacherous landslide! After all, those men must have come up that way.

He felt about for the handle of the door. It was a large iron ring. Jack twisted it this way and that, but the door did not open.

'That click I heard must have been the men locking it!' he thought angrily. 'It's impossible to get out. Blow it! Maybe if I'd been near enough I could have slipped out as they slipped in! It wouldn't have mattered if they had seen me because I could have run down the hillside before they could stop me!'

He sat and brooded near the door. 'I'll wait here in the shadows till they come back. Then I'll dash out with them. They'll be so taken by surprise that maybe they won't even put out a hand to me!'

So Jack sat there hour after hour, almost falling asleep. But the men did not return. Dinah could have told him why! They had gone through the secret door under the tapestry in the hidden room. The other three were somewhere in the castle.

When the eastern sky began to turn silver Jack knew it was time to return to his gorse bush. Kiki was fast asleep on his shoulder, having tired of the owl hours since. Button too had vanished.

Jack had not seen him go. He had forgotten about the little fox cub in the excitement of seeing the castle door open. He wondered where he had gone.

'I hope he's gone back to Tassie,' he thought. 'We can expect help sometime today if he has. About time too! I'm fed up with being here. Not an eagle left now, and the two girls in danger, to say nothing of poor old Philip. I wonder how he has got on. Perhaps the girls will tell me today.'

The girls came out of the hidden room about eight o'clock. The three men had gone down there and turned them out. Dinah had begged Philip to get back into the suit of armour before the men returned, but he wouldn't.

'No, I'd rather be under the bed,' he said firmly. 'One day in that horrible stiff suit is enough for me. I'd rather be caught than stand there all day again. You put me some food and drink under the bed, and I'll stay here. I can always wander about and stretch my legs when the men are not here.'

'Well – fortune favours the bold!' said Dinah, who thought that she would have felt the same if she had been Philip. 'It's a bold thing to do, to lie in hiding under the very bed the men may sleep on today – but maybe you'll be all right there. Don't sneeze, though!'

Apparently it was the men's intention to sleep the day away on the big four poster. They came down into the room and ordered the girls out. The bearded man flung himself on the bed. All the men looked tired, and the unshaven faces of the two were not nice to see.

'We'll call you down tonight,' said the bearded man, from the bed, and he yawned. 'Take what food you want from that pile of tins. There's a tin opener on the table. Now clear out and leave us. Couple of little nuisances!'

The girls grabbed a tin of sardines, a tin of salmon, one of peaches and one of apricots, and fled up the stairs. No sooner had they reached the top than the hole was closed by the stone.

'Sleep well!' said Dinah mockingly, and then the two girls went in search of Jack. He was under his gorse bush, wishing they would come.

'Jack! Are you all right? You can come out for a bit because the men are safe down in the underground room!' said Lucy-Ann. 'Do you want some sardines – or peaches? We've got both.'

'Hallo!' said Jack, delighted to see them. 'Is it really safe for a bit? All right, I'll come out and we'll squat behind this rock here. I'm longing for something to eat. Didn't you bring biscuits with you when you came yesterday?'

Dinah found the tin of biscuits, and they had a comic breakfast of sardines, biscuits and peaches, washed down by ginger beer. Still they all enjoyed it thoroughly, and exchanged their news eagerly.

Jack was intensely interested to hear all that Philip had told them. 'A secret way behind that tapestry!' he exclaimed, his eyes gleaming. 'But *where* does it lead to?'

'Goodness knows – into the hillside somewhere, I suppose,' said Dinah, dipping a biscuit into peach-juice and sucking it.

'Wait now – what side of the hidden room is the secret door in the wall?' asked Jack. 'Oh – opposite where Philip stood at the back – well, let me see – that means that the door would lead into the hill at the back of the castle. At the *back* of the castle! How funny! I wonder if there are dungeons there or something?'

'Oh dear – do you think the men are keeping people prisoners and perhaps starving them to death?' said Lucy-Ann, at once. 'Like that wicked old man did. Oh, Jack, you don't suppose that old man is still alive, do you, living like an old spider in his castle, still doing wicked things?'

'Of course not,' said Jack. 'Haven't I told you he's dead and gone years and years ago? Don't get such wild ideas into your head, Lucy-Ann. Now let me think a bit. Don't interrupt.'

He nibbled his biscuit and pondered again. 'Yes, I think I'm right,' he said. 'That door under the tapestry must lead underground through the hill at the back of the castle. I'd like to go down that passage and see what is there! I bet Philip will sooner or later!'

'I hope he'll be sensible and keep under the bed,' said Lucy-Ann. 'With men wandering in and out of secret doors and things, he might easily bump into one of them and be caught.'

'Did Button leave you last night?' said Dinah suddenly. 'Where is he?'

'Yes, he went at last,' said Jack. 'But where I don't know. I only hope he's found Tassie by now, and she has seen the note.'

'Philip says it won't be any good, that note,' said Lucy-Ann mournfully. 'We forgot that Tassie can't read.'

'Blow!' said Jack. 'Of course she can't. What silly-billies we are!'

'Silly-billy, silly-billy, silly-billy,' at once chanted Kiki, pleased. 'Pop goes the silly-billy!'

'You'll go pop in a minute if you eat any more peaches,' said Jack. 'Is the tin empty, Dinah? Put it away from Kiki, for goodness' sake. She's been tucking in like anything while we've been talking.'

'Poor old silly-billy,' said Kiki gloomily, as Dinah removed the tin and tapped her smartly on the beak.

'What are we going to do today?' said Lucy-Ann.

'Well, what *can* we do except wait?' said Jack.

'And hope that Tassie has the sense to show our note to someone,' said Dinah. 'Surely she would do that? She knows she can't get to us herself – or she *would* know, if she came, and saw the plank was gone!'

The day passed slowly. There was nothing to do, not even an eagle to watch. 'Wish I could do a spot of developing,' sighed Jack, feeling in his shorts pocket for his precious rolls of film. 'But I can't. I'm just longing to see how the eagles have come out.'

There was nothing to read. The girls wandered round a bit and wondered whether they dared to go up into the tower, and try to signal from there. But who would see? No one but Tassie, and she would not know what to make of the signals.

'Anyway, if you *did* go up into the tower, you might be badly punished by any of those men,' said Jack. 'It's not worth risking it. We must just wait in patience for Tassie to send help.'

The day passed at last and night came. The men yelled for the two girls to go down into the secret room again. They said a hurried goodnight to Jack and went. There was no question of disobeying the men. All the children were afraid of them.

Jack did not hide in his gorse bush. When it was dark enough he went down to the spring near the bottom of the wall, to get a drink. He dared not go into the kitchen for one, in case he bumped into one of the men, or they heard the pump clanking.

He bent down to the spring – and then listened in amazement. A most curious noise was coming from the little tunnel into which it disappeared.

'Oooph! Ow! Ooooph!' A scraping, dragging noise could be heard too. Something was coming up the tunnel. Jack stepped back in great alarm. Whatever could it be?

22

Tassie is very brave

Then Jack heard the unmistakable sound of Button yelping, and he knew that part of the noise must be made by the fox cub. He bent over the tunnel, and flashed his torch on to see down its narrow mouth.

He saw a white face staring up at him, and he jumped. It was Tassie's. She was lying still for the moment, but began to wriggle again when the light flashed on her.

'Tassie! What are you doing? Tassie!' said Jack, in a low but most astonished voice.

Tassie didn't answer. She squeezed herself up a bit more, until her head and shoulders were outside the tunnel. Then Jack gave her a pull and she came out at once. Button followed, looking very forlorn. Tassie had him on a lead, and he couldn't get away.

Tassie sat down and gasped painfully. She put her head over her knees, which were drawn up, and seemed quite unable to speak a word. Jack flashed his torch over her. She was soaking wet and unspeakably dirty. Mud streaked her face and arms and legs.

She was shivering with cold and fright. Jack made her get up and go with him to the crag. He put her behind a rock, and fetched the rugs. He made her strip off the soaked dress she wore, and cover herself from head to foot with a couple of rugs. Then the boy sat close to her to warm her. Kiki perched on her shoulder and pressed against her cold cheek. Soon Tassie's breath grew more even, and she turned to look at Jack, trying to summon up a faint smile.

'Where's Philip?' she whispered at last.

'With the girls,' said Jack, not wanting to tell her everything at once. 'Don't worry for a minute or two. Get your breath back. You're exhausted.'

He sat with his arm round her, feeling the pounding of her heart shaking her body. Poor Tassie! How had she managed to get so exhausted?

But she soon recovered, as her body grew warm. She pressed against Jack. 'I'm so hungry,' she said.

Jack fed her with biscuits and salmon from the tin. Then she drank the rest of the peach-juice, whilst Kiki copied the gulping noises she made.

'Now I feel better,' she said. 'What has been happening, Jack?'

'Well, suppose you tell me a few things first,' said the boy. 'And keep your voice low. There are enemies about.'

This was news to Tassie. Her eyes widened and she looked round, scared. 'Is it that wicked old man?' she whispered.

'Of course not,' said Jack. 'Tassie, did Button take you our note?'

'Yes, said Tassie. 'But, Jack, I gave my mother the slip and came up here yesterday to spend a few hours with you – and oh, Jack, the plank was gone. Where's it gone?'

'That's just what *I* should like to know!' said Jack grimly. 'Well, what did you do then?'

'I went back home,' said Tassie. 'And I was worried about you. Then this morning Button came to find me, and I saw his string collar, and the letter someone had tied to it.'

'Go on,' said Jack.

'Well – I couldn't read it,' said Tassie, with tears in her voice. 'And there was nobody to ask. My mother was angry with me, and Mrs Mannering had gone away. I didn't like to go to the farm with it – so I suddenly thought I would make a lead for Button, and when next he went up to the castle to look for Philip, I would go with him, and find the way he went.'

'That was clever!' said Jack admiringly. Tassie felt pleased.

'So I found an old dog lead,' she said, more cheerfully, 'and I fastened it to his collar, and I went wherever he went that day. He was awfully angry about it. He kept trying to bite the lead, and he almost tried to bite me too!'

Jack patted the little fox cub who was lying quietly beside them. 'He didn't understand what was happening,' he said. 'Well – he brought you up here at last, I suppose?'

'Yes. After he had wandered for miles on the hillside, and almost worn me out, going up and down, up and down!' said Tassie. 'When it was dark he decided to come and look for Philip again – and he shot off like an arrow then!'

'I bet he did,' said Jack. 'Poor old Button – he must wonder where Philip has gone to!'

'Well, he dragged me behind on the lead,' said Tassie, 'and brought me all the way up beside the spring. Below the castle it goes into a narrow sort of tunnel – terribly narrow in parts – and oh, Jack, it goes right underneath the wall! Think of that! And comes up the other side!'

'Did you really wriggle all the way?' said Jack, in amazement. 'What a marvel you are, Tassie! But didn't the water pour down on you all the time?'

'Oh yes – it nearly choked me sometimes,' said Tassie. 'And it was so icy-cold! But most of the way up the spring the tunnel wasn't too bad – it was through rock, and it had worn it away, so that the water ran in a kind of channel in the rock, and there was space for me to wriggle up more easily. It was at the beginning and at the end, where it comes up in the castle yard, that it was so narrow. Once I thought I was really stuck! I couldn't go up and I couldn't go down – and I thought I might have to stay there for ever, because no one would ever know where I was!'

'Poor Tassie!' said Jack, giving her a hug. 'You're a very brave girl. Wait till Philip hears about this! He'll think you are wonderful.'

Tassie glowed with delight. She hoped Philip would be pleased with her. She had come to help them. And now, in her turn, she questioned Jack eagerly, wanting to know everything that had happened to her four friends since they had left her.

Jack told her the story. She listened in alarm and astonishment. Philip hiding in a suit of old armour – down in a hidden room – the girls prisoners there – cruel men wandering about furtively, nobody knew why – secret passages – why, it was like a dream! But at least here was Jack with Kiki, safe and sound!

'Could you wriggle down the tunnel with me, and we'll fetch help?' said Tassie.

'That's just what I thought of doing,' said Jack. 'I think I'd better go tonight, Tassie, and not wait to take the two girls. Anyway I'm afraid there would be more risk of someone getting stuck in that watery tunnel. I'd better go and get help as soon as possible. You'd better stay here and tell the girls what has happened. You can hide in my old gorse bush till they come tomorrow morning.'

Tassie sighed with relief. She did not in the least want to go back down that terrible way again. She would dream about it all her life long! Neither did she really want to stay in the courtyard alone for the night, but Jack said he would leave both Kiki and Button with her, and they could sleep in the gorse bush all together.

'So you be brave and do that,' he said. 'Maybe you'll see Philip tomorrow too. He *will* be surprised to hear your adventures!'

Tassie, still clad in the rugs, went with Jack to the place near the wall, where the bubbling spring ran into the beginning of the tunnel. Jack marvelled how anyone could wriggle down much less wriggle *up*, with water splashing into his face all the time.

'Now, you go straight back to the bush with Button and Kiki, wrap yourself up warmly in the rugs, and go to sleep,' said Jack. 'Don't let Kiki see me disappearing down here, or she'll want to follow me.'

So Tassie obediently went back to the gorse bush and crawled inside. She curled up in the rugs like a little animal, with Button on her feet and Kiki perched on her middle, waiting for Jack. Tassie hoped Kiki would not fly off when she found Jack did not come. She might make a dreadful noise if she found he had disappeared!

Jack crawled head-first into the cold water. He wriggled into the tunnel. It smelt damp and nasty. He dragged his body down, using hands and elbows to lever himself along. It wasn't at all pleasant.

'I wish Button had found some better way of getting into the castle and out!' thought the boy. 'How *could* Tassie have crawled up, with the water splashing into her face half the time? She's really a heroine!'

When he had got down some way, the rather earthy tunnel gave way to hard rock. Jack thought he must be under the wall by now. The tunnel widened out considerably, and the boy sat on a ledge to rest. He was worried about his rolls of film. He had wrapped them up very carefully in a sou'wester one of the children had brought up to the castle, and had tied the strings round tightly. It would be too sickening if his precious films were spoilt.

He began to shiver with the cold, for he was now soaked through. As long as he was dragging himself along the tunnel he was warm, for it was very hard work – but as soon as he stopped, the cold got him, and he shook like a leaf.

He went on again. It was quite dark, and he could only feel his way along. He went on wriggling down the watery passage, glad when it was wide and high, anxious when it closed in on his body, and made it difficult for him to get along.

It seemed hours before he reached the outlet, but at last he was there! He dragged himself out, and sat panting on a patch of soft heather. He hoped that never in his life again would he have to crawl through a tunnel like that! He was sure that if the girls had been with him, someone would have got stuck with fright, and would not have been able to go either up or down, after a while. It was just as well that he had decided they must not all use this way of escape.

He began to shiver, and he stood up, his knees shaking after his long ordeal underground. He was not as exhausted as Tassie, but he was almost tired out.

'I shall get an awful chill if I don't get warm,' he thought, and he set off down the hill, glad of the bright moonlight.

He stumbled along, looking eagerly for a sight of Spring Cottage as he at last dropped down into the lane that led to it. Yes – there it was, black with the moonlight behind it, its roof silvered and shining.

Then suddenly Jack stopped. He had seen something that struck him as odd.

'There's smoke – smoke coming from the chimney!' he

said to himself, and he leaned against a tree. 'What does that mean? Can Aunt Allie be back? No, Tassie would have known. Well, then – who has lighted the kitchen fire? Who is there? Oh, surely one of those wretched men hasn't gone there to find out something about the girls?'

He crept near to the cottage. He came to the little garden. There was a light shining out of one of the windows!

Jack tiptoed to the window, anxious and puzzled. He looked cautiously in. Someone was sitting in a tall-backed armchair that had its back to Jack. Was it Mrs Mannering?

A cloud of smoke suddenly came from the chair – thick blue pipe-smoke!

'It's a man,' whispered Jack to himself. 'Whoever can it be?'

23

A few surprises

Jack stayed at the window, shivering. If only the man would get up – then he could see if it was one of the men he knew at the castle. But how dare he get into the house like that!

Jack made up his mind to creep into the house and peep through the crack in the kitchen door. Then he would be able to see who it was sitting in the armchair. So, still shivering, as much with excitement as with cold, he stole round to the other side of the house, where his bedroom window was. If it was open, Jack knew he could climb the tree near by and slip inside.

It *was* open – just a crack. But Jack remembered that the catch was very loose, and he could probably put in his hand and jiggle it off the iron peg that held it down. It was a casement window and would open very wide to let him in.

He stumbled over a bucket or something outside a door, and stopped still, wondering if the man inside had heard anything. Then on he went to the tree, and climbed it quickly.

He slipped his hand inside the crack of the window and jiggled the catch. It dropped, and the window swung open. Jack cautiously climbed inside, and stood there, hardly daring to breathe.

He made his way into the dark little passage between the bedrooms, and stood there, waiting for a moment before he ventured down the rather creaky, winding stairs. Then he began to go down, one step at a time, hoping to goodness they wouldn't creak too loudly.

There was a bend in one place, and Jack meant to stand there quietly before he went on – but no sooner had he got there than someone leapt on him, caught his arms, and jerked him violently down the last four stairs! He fell, and all the breath was bumped out of his body.

Whoever had jumped on him stood up and then pulled him roughly to his feet. Then he was propelled swiftly into the lighted kitchen, and he looked at once to the armchair to see who was there.

But it was empty! Whoever had sat there must have heard him, and lain in wait for him. Jack turned to face his captor, wriggling, fully expecting to see one of the men from the tower.

The two stared at one another in the very greatest surprise, and stepped backwards in amazement.

'Bill Smugs!'

'Jack! What on *earth* are you doing creeping in like this? I thought you must be a burglar!'

'Golly! You've bruised me properly,' said Jack, rubbing himself. He began to shiver violently again. Bill looked at his soaking clothes and pale face, and pulled him to the fire, on which a kettle was boiling merrily.

'What *have* you been up to? You're dripping wet! You'll

get a frightful chill. Where are the others? When I arrived today to ask Mrs Mannering if she could put me up for a night or two, the house was shut, and there was no one here!'

'Well, how did you get in, then?' asked Jack, enjoying the warmth of the fire.

'Oh, I have my ways,' said Bill. 'I thought you must all have gone picnicking, so I waited and waited for you to come back – but you didn't. So I decided to spend the night here by myself, and make enquiries somewhere tomorrow to see what had happened to you all. Then I heard mysterious sounds, decided it was a burglar – and caught *you*!'

'Well, I looked in at the window, and couldn't see who was sitting in that chair, so I thought I'd creep in and have a squint round,' said Jack. 'Oh, Bill, I'm glad to see you. We're in danger!'

'What do you mean?' said Bill, astonished. 'Where are the girls? And Philip?'

'It's a long story, but I must tell you from the very beginning,' said Jack. 'What about a hot drink whilst we are talking, Bill. I could do with one. That kettle's on the boil.'

'I was about to make the same remark myself,' said Bill. 'Hot cocoa and biscuits for you, I think! I'm glad you've stopped shivering. By the way, where's Mrs Mannering? Don't tell me she's in danger too!'

'Oh no – she's gone off to look after Philip's Aunt Polly, who is ill again,' said Jack. 'She's all right.'

Bill made a jug of hot cocoa and milk, found some biscuits, and gave them to Jack, who was now feeling a lot warmer. He had stripped off his wet things, and was sitting in a dressing-gown.

'I don't feel I ought to waste time like this, really,' he said, 'as the others are in danger. But I'll have to tell you the whole story, and then leave it to you what to do.'

'Go ahead,' said Bill.

So Jack began, and Bill listened in the greatest interest and astonishment. He burst into laughter at Philip's idea of hiding in the suit of armour.

'Just like old Philip! What a good idea! The men would never guess anyone was hiding there.'

He grew serious as the tale went on. He pulled at his pipe and kept his eyes fixed on Jack. His ruddy face grew even redder in the fire-light, and the bald top of his head gleamed and shone.

'This is an extraordinary tale, Jack,' he said at last. 'There is a lot more in this than you know. What were those men like? Describe them. Was there a man with a scar right across his chin and neck?'

'No,' said Jack, thinking. 'Not one of them as far as I know. I took a jolly good snap of one man, though – when they were at the eagles' nest. You know I told you I had my camera poking out of the gorse bush to snap the eagles. Well, I snapped him when one of the eagles flew at him. I snapped both men, as a matter of fact, but one unfortunately had his face turned away.'

'Have you got those snaps?' said Bill eagerly.

'I've got the films,' said Jack, and he pointed to the tightly rolled up sou'wester on the table. 'They're in there. They're not developed yet, Bill.'

'Well, whilst you have a good sleep, I'll develop them,' said Bill. 'I see you've got a little darkroom fixed up for yourself off the hall there, where you meant to do developing – you've got everything necessary there, haven't you?'

'But – but – oughtn't we go right back and rescue the girls?' asked Jack.

'I shall have to drive over to the town where you met me the other day,' said Bill, 'and collect a few men, and arrange a few things. If these men are doing what I think they are, then we stand a good chance of roping them all in together. I don't think they will harm the girls at all.'

'What are the men doing?' asked Jack curiously. 'Are they anything to do with the job you said you were on, Bill?'

'Can't tell you yet,' said Bill. 'I hardly think so – but I shall soon know.' He paused and looked at Jack.

'What children you are for falling headlong into adventures!' he said. 'I never knew anyone like you for that! It seems to me I'd better stick close to you all the year round, and then I shall have a good chance of sharing them!'

He put Jack on the sofa, arranged rugs over him, turned down the lamp, and went off into the little darkroom with the films. Jack had shown him which roll contained the snap of the man.

Jack slept peacefully, for he was tired out. How long he slept he didn't know, but he was awakened by Bill coming into the room in the greatest excitement, holding a film.

'Sorry to wake you, Jack – but this is a marvellous thing!' he said, and held up the film to the daylight, which was now coming in at the window. 'You have snapped this man perfectly – every detail is as clear as could be. He's the man with the beard – but just look here! He is holding his head up, and the whole of his neck is exposed from chin to chest, because his collar has flapped open. What can you see?'

'A mark – like a long scar,' said Jack, sitting up.

'Quite right!' said Bill. He took out a notebook from his pocket, slipped a snap from it and showed it to Jack. 'Look there – see that scar on that man's chin and neck?'

Jack saw a clean-shaven man in the photograph, his chin and neck disfigured by a terrible scar.

'That's the same man, though you wouldn't think it, because in your snap he wears a black beard, which he has probably grown lately. But the scar on the neck still gives him away, if his collar happens to be open – and it was, in your snap! Now I know for certain what those men in the castle are up to. I've been looking for this fellow for six months!'

'Who is he?' asked Jack curiously.

'His name, his *real* name is Mannheim,' said Bill, 'but he is known as Scar-Neck. He is a very dangerous spy.'

'Golly!' said Jack, staring. 'Were you after him?'

'Well, I was detailed to keep an eye on him and watch his movements,' said Bill. 'I wasn't to capture him because we wanted to know what he was up to this time, and who his friends were. Then we hoped to rope in the whole lot. But Scar-Neck is a very clever fellow with an absolute gift for disappearing. I traced him to the town where you met me – and then I lost him completely.'

'He went to the castle!' said Jack. 'What a wonderful hiding place!'

'I should rather like to know the real history of that castle,' said Bill thoughtfully. 'I must enquire into its ownership. Do you know what is on the other side of the hill, Jack?'

'No,' said Jack, puzzled. 'We've never been there. Why?'

'I just wondered if you had heard anyone talking,' said Bill. 'I can't tell you any more now. My word, I am glad I bumped into you the other day, and came on here to look you up!'

'So am I, Bill,' said Jack. 'I simply didn't know what I was going to do! Now you're here, and I can leave the whole thing to you.'

'You can,' said Bill. 'Now I'm off in the car to the town, to do a little reporting on the telephone there, and to collect a few friends, and one or two necessary things. You go to sleep again till I come back. I promise you I won't be a minute longer than I can help.'

Jack settled back on the sofa again. 'I don't think I've caught a chill after all,' he said. 'What a lucky thing for me you had a fire, Bill!'

'Well, there was nothing else to boil a kettle with!' said Bill. 'So I had to light one. No, I don't think you're going to get a chill either. You'll be able to go up to the castle with me when I come back, and show me the way.'

'But how will we get in!' called Jack, as Bill went out to get his car. There was no reply except the sound of the car being started up.

'I can leave everything to Bill,' thought Jack. 'Golly, I wonder what will happen now!'

24

Kiki gives a performance

Up in the castle courtyard Tassie passed an exciting night. She had tried to go to sleep in the middle of the gorse bush, and had fallen into a doze, when Kiki began to get restless. She dug her claws into Tassie, and woke her up.

'Don't, Kiki,' said Tassie sleepily. 'Keep still, do!'

But Kiki was waiting for Jack, and couldn't make out why he hadn't come back. She began to murmur to herself, and Tassie reached out a hand and tapped her on the beak.

'Be quiet, Kiki! Do go to sleep! Button is as good as gold.'

There was a sound in the courtyard outside. Kiki put her head on one side, and listened. She thought it was Jack.

'Put the kettle on!' she cried joyfully, and scrambled out from the bush. 'Put the kettle on!'

There was an astonished silence in the yard below. Then a torch was switched on, and its powerful beam swept round. But Kiki was behind a rock and could not be seen.

Two men were down in the yard. They had heard Kiki's

voice, and, not knowing there was a parrot about, they thought it was someone talking.

'Wipe your feet!' called Kiki. 'How many times have I told you to wipe your feet?'

The men began to talk together in low voices, planning to capture whoever it was calling in such a loud voice. Kiki began to realise that it was not Jack down there, and she was disappointed and cross.

'Pop goes the weasel,' she said in a mournful voice. One of the men stooped down in the darkness, felt about for a stone, and sent it whizzing in Kiki's direction. The parrot would certainly have been killed if the stone had hit it. But it missed by about an inch.

Kiki was startled. No one had ever thrown a stone at her in her life. She spread her wings and flew up to the wall behind the men.

'Naughty boy!' she said reprovingly, 'naughty, naughty boy!'

The men gave cries of fury, and swung round, trying in vain to see who was now on the wall. They thought there must be two people now, one up on the crag, and the other on the wall.

'You come down,' said one of the men threateningly. 'We've got you covered! We're not standing any more of this nonsense!'

'Fusty, musty, dusty!' chanted Kiki, and then flew down into the courtyard, just behind the men. They were in darkness and so was she.

Kiki growled like a dog, and the men jumped in fright. The sound was just behind them.

'There's a dog about too,' said one of the men. 'Look out! Shoot, if you like!'

The frightened man pressed the trigger of the revolver he was carrying, and the sound of the shot cracked out in the night, making Tassie, in the gorse bush, jump almost out of her skin. Button, too, leapt with fright and ran out of the bush.

He still had his lead on. He ran down into the courtyard, and his lead dragged after him. As he ran by the men the lead touched one of them, and he fired again. Button yelped, though he was not hit, and the man switched on his torch. He caught sight of the cub slinking away.

'Was that the dog?' he said. 'It's a mighty small one.'

Kiki was enjoying herself. She flew to a tree near by, and began to mew. She could mew just as well as she could bark. The men listened to this new sound in the greatest surprise.

'Cats now,' said one. 'I can't understand it! There never seems anything here in the daytime. Is it children having a joke?'

'God save the King, silly-billy, silly-billy,' said Kiki from the tree, and went off into one of her cackling laughs. Then she clucked like a hen, and finished up with an eagle's yelping scream. It was a very fine performance, but the men didn't like it at all.

'Let's go back inside,' said one of them nervously. 'This place is bewitched. It's all voices and noises but nothing much to show for them. Let's go back.'

Kiki let off one of her express train screeches, and that finished the men completely. They ran for the castle as if an engine was about to run them down! Kiki laughed again, and her cackle sounded very eerie in the dark courtyard. Even Tassie felt frightened, though she knew it was only Kiki.

There was peace after that. Kiki, after flying round a little while to look for Jack, came back to the old gorse bush and struggled inside to join Tassie.

The little girl was glad of her company. 'Button's gone,' she said to Kiki. 'I expect he's gone down that watery tunnel again. Now, Kiki, settle down and go to sleep. I'm so very tired.'

This time Kiki did settle down. She put her head under her wing, gave a little sigh, and went to sleep. Tassie too slept, and there was complete silence except for the trickling noise made by the spring in the corner of the yard.

Tassie was wakened by Dinah and Lucy-Ann. They had passed quite a peaceful night down in the hidden room, undisturbed this time, with Philip on the floor under the bed. He was getting very tired of living underground, and wanted to make a dash for it with the girls. But Dinah persuaded him that that would be dangerous for him, and make things even worse for them. So, grumbling, he had resumed his place under the big bed, where the girls had also put a good supply of food.

'Jack!' said Lucy-Ann, in a low voice, as she came to the bush. 'Jack! Are you there?'

Jack was not there, of course, but Lucy-Ann didn't know that. Tassie awoke and sat up, pricking herself against the bush.

'Jack!' said Lucy-Ann again, and parted the bush to see inside. 'Oh – *you*, Tassie! How did *you* get here?'

Tassie grinned. She was feeling quite all right again after a night's rest. Her face looked dreadful. It was muddy and scratched, and her hair was a wild mass of muddy tangles. She had put on her old dress once more.

'Hallo,' said Tassie. 'I came to help you. I got your note, but I couldn't read it. So I came up to see what it was all about. But the plank was gone. So I found out where Button came in and out, and came with him!'

'Did you really?' said Dinah. 'Where did Button get in, Tassie?'

Tassie told her. The girls listened in surprise. 'How could you crawl up a horrid, wet tunnel like that?' said Lucy-Ann, shuddering at the thought. 'Tassie, you are marvellous, you really are! I could never do that, I know I couldn't.'

'I don't believe I could either,' said Dinah. 'It was wonderful of you, Tassie.'

Tassie felt pleased, and smiled at the two girls. It was nice to be praised like this.

'But where's Jack?' asked Lucy-Ann.

'Gone down the tunnel to get help,' said Tassie. 'He said I was to tell you he was sorry to go without saying goodbye, but he thought it best to go at once.'

'Oh,' said Lucy-Ann, her face falling in dismay. 'I wish he hadn't gone without me.'

'Well, you know you've just said that you couldn't possibly go down that tunnel,' said Dinah. 'I'm jolly glad you came up, Tassie, so that Jack knew the way to escape. He'll get help and bring somebody up here, I'm sure. That's good!'

'But how will they get in?' asked Lucy-Ann.

'They could bring a plank again, couldn't they?' said Tassie.

Kiki joined in the conversation. 'Don't sniff,' she said amiably. 'Where's your handkerchief?'

'Oh, Kiki was so funny last night!' said Tassie, remembering, and told the two girls what had happened. When she described how the men had shot at Kiki, Lucy-Ann looked alarmed.

'Gracious! They are very dangerous men!' she said. 'I don't like them. I want to escape too. I think I'll crawl down that horrid tunnel after all, Dinah. You come too, and Tassie as well. We'll all go.'

'What, and leave Philip all alone here?' cried Tassie indignantly. 'You go if you like, but I shan't.'

'Yes, of course – we can't leave Philip,' said Dinah. 'Oh, Tassie, do come and wash your face. It's simply awful. You look like a sweep. And your clothes! Gracious, they're filthy, and all in rags.'

'I couldn't help it,' said Tassie. 'It was awful in that tunnel. I kept getting caught on things. I'll come and wash if you think it's safe.'

'Well – I suppose it isn't, really,' said Dinah, thinking about it. 'The men might come out and see you, and know you're not one of us two. We'll bring you some water, and you can clean yourself up, outside the bush.'

'Then we'll all have breakfast,' said Lucy-Ann, who was hungry.

It was difficult to get Tassie clean, because all they had to bring water in was an empty ginger beer bottle and a cardboard cup. But by means of a couple of handkerchiefs and the water, she did manage to clean her face and hands a bit. Then they ate breakfast.

Kiki ate breakfast with them. Of Button there was no sign. They thought he must have gone down the tunnel some time in the night, and was probably with Jack again.

'Look – there are the eagles back again!' said Dinah suddenly. Tassie looked round with interest, for she had not seen them that morning. The three birds came dropping down to the ledge, and sat there, looking regally out on the courtyard.

'The young one flies as well as the older birds now, doesn't he?' said Lucy-Ann, and threw him a biscuit. But he didn't even give it a look! He continued his impassive stare, appearing to be frowning deeply.

'I wish Jack was here. He would like to snap them all together like that,' said Lucy-Ann. 'His camera is still in the bush, but I don't like to use it. I suppose it's all right there if it rains, Dinah?'

'It doesn't look as if it will rain,' said Dinah. But Tassie disagreed.

'It feels stormy,' she said. 'I think there will be a thunderstorm, and maybe torrents of rain. I hope we shan't be here, on the top of the hill, if there is a storm, because it would be a frightening sight. The thunder rolls round and round the top, and the lightning seems to run down the hillside!'

'I expect we'll all be rescued before the storm comes,' said Dinah. 'I'm expecting to see Jack any time now – bringing us help of some sort!'

25

At midnight

Jack slept peacefully again for some hours. He did not wake till Bill returned in the car. With him were four 'friends'. Jack thought they looked pretty tough. It was plain that Bill was in authority over them.

Bill came into the kitchen, leaving the men outside. 'Hallo!' he said. 'Awake at last? Do you want a meal? It's gone one o'clock.'

'Gracious, is it!' said Jack. 'Yes, I feel jolly hungry.'

'You get up now and put some clothes on,' said Bill, 'and I'll call one of my men in to fix us up a meal. I don't expect Mrs Mannering will mind if we make free with her kitchen today.'

'Are we going up to the castle soon?' said Jack, gathering the dressing-gown round him, and preparing to go upstairs to his bedroom.

'Not till tonight,' said Bill. 'The moon won't be up till late, and we plan to go just before midnight, whilst it is still dark. I've no doubt one or other of those men keep a lookout during the daytime.'

'Oh – the girls will be awfully tired of waiting for us, all day long,' said Jack.

'Can't very well help it,' said Bill. 'It is most important

that we get in without being seen.'

Jack went up and dressed. It was terribly hot, though the sun was behind sulky-looking clouds. He felt out of breath, though he had done nothing at all.

'Feels like a storm,' he thought. 'I hope it won't come today. It might frighten the girls up there all alone.'

There was a scampering of clawed feet on the stairs, and into his bedroom came Button, his brush waving behind him, his sharp eyes fixed on Jack as if to say 'Well, well, how you do get about, to be sure! I never know whether to find you up at the castle or down here – but I wish I could find old Philip!'

'Looking for Tufty, are you?' said Jack, patting the fox cub, who immediately rolled over like a dog. 'Hey, Bill – did you see our fox cub?'

'Well, a small tornado swept into the kitchen and up the stairs,' called back Bill, 'but I didn't see what it was! Come on down with him.'

Jack went down, carrying Button, who licked his nose rapturously all the time. Bill thought he was fine.

They had a meal together, and Bill asked a good many questions about the castle and the men, and the hidden room, which Jack answered as clearly as he could. He was certain that Bill meant to enter the castle somehow, and capture the men – but he couldn't see how it was to be done.

'They looked pretty dangerous fellows,' he said to Bill. 'I mean – they're probably well armed.'

'Don't worry – they won't be the only ones,' said Bill grimly. 'I know Scar-Neck of old – he doesn't usually leave anything to chance. He must have been pretty fed up when he found the girls in his precious hidden room! I guess their being there has made him hurry up his plans a bit, whatever they are.'

Jack began to feel excited. 'This adventure is boiling up,' he said, in a pleased tone.

'Yes. And somebody is going to get badly scalded,' said Bill.

Jack developed his other films. The snaps came out marvellously! The eagles stood out well, almost every feather showing clearly. The baby eagle was the star turn. Its poses were perfect.

'Look at these, Bill,' said Jack, thrilled.

'My word – they're really striking!' said Bill admiringly. 'You ought to get those taken by any first-class magazine, Jack. They would pay well for them too! You'll soon make a name for yourself, at this rate.'

Jack felt proud. If he could make a name for himself through the birds he loved, he would be happy. He wondered how Kiki was getting on without him. How disgusted she would be when she found that he was gone! Never mind – Tassie was there, and she was very fond of her.

The day dragged a little. After tea Jack felt sleepy, and Bill told him to have a nap.

'You had an awful night – and as we shall want your help tonight, you'd better sleep for a few hours. Then you will be wide awake.'

So Jack curled up on a rug in the garden outside and slept. It was hot and sultry there. Bill's men, who had sat playing cards with one another all day long, and had hardly spoken a word, removed their coats, and then their shirts. It was almost too hot to breathe.

Jack awoke again before it was dark. He went to find Bill. 'Oughtn't we to start now?' he said. 'It takes a bit of time to get up the hill.'

'We're going as far as we can by car,' said Bill. 'These fellows are tough, but they don't like mountain climbing! We'll follow the road till we get to the landslide, and then climb the rest of the way.'

Just as it got dark they all piled into Bill's big car and set off up the hill. The car seemed to make rather a noise, Jack thought, but Bill assured him it wouldn't be heard at the castle.

'The only thing that worries me a bit is having Philip down in that hidden room,' said Bill. 'If there's a rough house down there – and I rather think there may be – I don't want kids mixed up in it.'

'Well, really – Bill – it was us kids who got *you* mixed up in this adventure!' said Jack, most indignantly.

'Yes, I know,' said Bill, with a laugh. 'But it rather cramps our style to have you around just now!'

'Bill, what are you going to do?' asked Jack, with curiosity. 'Do tell me. You might as well!'

'I'm not quite sure,' said Bill. 'It depends on how things turn out. But roughly the plan is this – to get down into that hidden room tonight, when the girls are there, we hope, and the men are not. . . .'

'Set the girls free!' said Jack. 'And Philip too, can't you?'

'Yes – if Philip will condescend to scoot off with the girls!' said Bill. 'But we want him to show us the secret way under the tapestry first, and I have an idea that he will want to come with us then!'

'I bet he will,' said Jack. 'So shall I, I don't mind telling you! I'm not going to be left out of this now, if I can help it.'

'I want to find out where that secret door leads to,' said Bill. 'I think I know, but I want to make sure. And I want to learn a few things without those men at the castle knowing it. It was a pity they spoke in a language Philip couldn't understand or he might have learnt what we want to know!'

'Well, how are *you* going to learn it, then?' asked Jack.

'Same way as Philip might have!' said Bill, with a laugh. 'Put myself and the men into those suits of armour, and listen in to the conversation!'

'Gosh!' said Jack, thrilled. 'I never thought of that. Oh, Bill – do you really think you can do that? Can Philip and I hide too?'

'We'll see,' said Bill. 'I thought it was a mighty good idea of Philip's to hide in that armour, I must say, even though it was only for a joke at first. Now – here we are at the landslide, surely?'

They were. They all had to get out, and Jack now had to lead the way. He found the narrow rabbit-path they had so often used, and led the men along it, using his torch as he did so, because it was not easy in the darkness to pick out the right path.

They all walked in dead silence, in obedience to an order from Bill. Button the fox cub ran at Jack's heels, suddenly hopeful of seeing Philip. An owl called near by and made them all jump.

It was so hot that everyone panted, and rubbed wet foreheads. Jack's shirt stuck to him. There was a rumble of thunder far away in the distance.

'I thought there was a storm coming,' said Jack to himself, wiping his forehead for the twentieth time, to stop the perspiration dripping into his eyes. 'I hope the girls are safely down in that underground room. Then they won't hear the storm. But I suppose they'll have to leave poor little Tassie up in the courtyard, because they won't dare to let the men see her. Or Kiki. I hope they're both all right.'

They went on upwards, and at last came to the great castle wall. Jack stopped.

'Here's the castle wall,' he whispered. 'How are you going to get into the castle, Bill?'

'Where's that other door you told me of – not the big front door that overlooks the landslide, and which the men came in by – the other, smaller door, somewhere in the wall of the castle?' asked Bill.

'I'll take you to it – but I told you it was locked,' said Jack. He led Bill and the others round the wall, turned a corner, and came to the door.

It was very stout and strong, made of solid oak, set flush

with the wall. The wall arched above it, and the door arched too. Bill took out his torch and flashed it quickly up and down the door, coming to a stop at the lock.

He beckoned to one of the men. The fellow came up, and brought out an amazing collection of keys from his pocket. Deftly and silently he fitted first one and then another into the keyhole. Not one of them turned the lock.

'No good, sir,' he whispered to Bill. 'This isn't an old lock – it's a special one, fitted quite recently. I shan't be able to open it with any of my keys.'

Jack listened in disappointment. Surely this did not mean that they would have to batter the door in? That would certainly give warning to the men.

Bill sent for one of the other men. He came up with a curious thing in his hand, rather like a small can with a thick spout. Jack stared at it, wondering what it was.

'You'll have to get to work on it, Jim,' said Bill. 'Go ahead. Make as little noise as possible. Stop if I nudge you.'

A sizzling noise came from the can, and a jet of strong blue flame shot out from the spout, making Jack jump. The man pointed the spout of flame at the door, just above the lock.

Jack watched, fascinated. The curious blue flame ate away the wood completely! What kind of fire they were using Jack didn't know, but it was very powerful. Quietly the man worked with his can of flame, holding it steadily over the wood that surrounded the lock. The flame ate away a gap at the top of the lock. It ate away the side of it. And then it ate away the wood below the lock.

Now Jack saw what was happening to the door! The man had managed to isolate the lock completely, so that the door would swing open easily, leaving the lock behind! The boy thought it was a very clever idea.

'Now to go in,' said Bill, as he swung the door slowly open. 'Everyone ready?'

26

Going into hiding

They filed in silently. The last man shut the door, and wedged in a bit of wood by the lock to keep it from swinging. The courtyard was beginning to get light, because the moon was rising, though it was behind the clouds most of the time.

'I'll just go and see if Tassie is under my gorse bush,' whispered Jack. 'We'll have to find out the latest news from her, and she'll have to escape with the girls too, as soon as possible. She can guide them back to Spring Cottage.'

The men waited in the shadows with Bill whilst Jack went over to the crag. He climbed up to the gorse bush. A loud voice hailed him.

'Put the kettle on! How many times have I . . .'

'Shut up, Kiki,' whispered Jack, in a panic. He heard someone stirring in the bush and called in a low voice.

'Is that you, Tassie? It's Jack, back again!'

Tassie crawled out of the bush, full of joy, for she had been feeling frightened and lonely.

'Oh, Jack! Did you come up that awful watery tunnel like I did? Did you get help?'

'Yes – Bill Smugs is here – with some of his men,' whispered Jack. 'You and the other two girls must go down to Spring Cottage. Philip and I are going to wait and see what happens – if Bill will let us!'

'But how can you get the girls?' asked Tassie. 'You know they are down in the hidden room, with Philip.'

'Easy,' said Jack. 'We'll just pull the spike in the wall at the back of the hall, and get them out! Then, Tassie, you and they must hurry off as quickly as you can.'

'I'd like to stay with Philip,' said Tassie obstinately. 'And anyway, there's going to be a dreadful storm. I don't want to go down the hillside with thunder and lightning all round me.'

'Well – you'll have to do as Bill tells you,' said Jack. 'Maybe you'll get down before the storm comes. Are the girls all right, Tassie?'

'Yes, but rather tired of it,' said Tassie. 'Oh, Jack, Kiki made a simply awful noise last night after you had gone, and the men heard her – and they shot at her! I was really frightened!'

'Golly!' said Jack. 'I'm glad *you* weren't hit, Tassie! You might easily have been wounded.'

'The girls went down into the secret room when the men called out to them this evening,' said Tassie. 'But they asked them all kinds of questions, in horrid, rough voices. They couldn't understand Kiki talking last night, you see, and thought there must be someone else here that we hadn't told them about. So, in the end, Dinah had to tell them it was Kiki the parrot – and after that they didn't worry them any more.'

'Come on – we must go over to Bill, and tell him all this,' said Jack. 'The men are waiting over there, look – Bill's men, I mean, of course!'

The moon struggled out as the two went over to the little group of silent men, so they kept in the shadows, fearful of being seen. It wouldn't do to give the game away to any watcher just at this critical moment.

'Where are the other men?' whispered Jack to Tassie. 'Do you know? Are they down in the hidden room – or wandering about the castle anywhere?'

'As far as I know they're not about the castle anywhere – or in the courtyard,' said Tassie. 'They may be down in the hidden room though. Won't you have to look out, if you press that spike and open the entrance?'

'Yes, we shall,' said Jack. 'Now here's Bill Smugs, our friend, Tassie. This is Tassie, Bill, the girl I was telling you about.'

Bill put a few questions to Tassie, and she answered them shyly. It rather looked as if the men were down in the secret room. Well – they would get a shock when the stone swung back, and they saw who were at the top of the steps!

'Now listen,' said Bill. 'You are to work the lever that opens the entrance to the secret room, Jack. One of my men will watch you, to see how you do it, in case we want to use it again. As soon as the entrance is open, I and the others will stand at the top and shout down to the men below to come up. We shall, I hope, have them covered with our revolvers!'

'Golly!' said Jack, a prickle of excitement running up and down his back. 'Look out for the girls, Bill. They may be scared stiff!'

'I can yell to them to keep out of the way,' said Bill. 'You leave things to me. I promise you the girls won't get hurt. We'll have them up the steps in no time – and you, Tassie, must take them straight away down the hill to Spring Cottage. Understand?'

'I'd like to stay with Philip,' Tassie still insisted.

'Well, you can't,' said Bill. 'You'll have Philip back with you tomorrow. Now – you all understand what's to be done?'

Everyone did. Quietly they all moved forward towards the great black hulk of the castle, lost in black shadows. The moon had gone behind thick clouds. A rumble of thunder came on the air again, still far away.

They stepped silently into the hall. Everyone but Tassie was wearing rubber shoes – Tassie, as usual, was barefoot. She hadn't even got her shoes tied round her neck or waist this time. She had hidden them, for her mother had threatened to take them away from her.

Jack slipped quietly to the back of the hall with one of the men. Tassie showed Bill the entrance to the underground room. He and the others waited there whilst Jack pulled back the spike in the wall. A grating noise was heard – and once again the stone swung back, and then sideways. A yawning hole appeared, with stone steps leading downwards.

The light from the lamp shone upwards. Bill stood at the top of the hole, listening intently. There was no sound at all from below.

Jack tiptoed up to him. 'Maybe there are only the girls and Philip there,' he whispered. 'Perhaps the men have gone off somewhere, down the secret way behind that tapestry.'

Bill nodded. He sent his voice rumbling down the hole. 'Who's down here? Answer!'

A small voice came back. It was Dinah's.

'Only us. Who's that?'

'Dinah! It's me and Bill Smugs!' called Jack, before Bill could stop him. 'Are you alone?'

'Yes,' came back Dinah's voice, lifted in excitement. 'Is *Bill* there? Oh, good!'

Jack ran down the steps, and Bill and the others followed, one man being left at the top on guard. The first thing Bill did was to find the spike in the wall down below, and close up the hole. He waited a moment, and then the man at the top, as arranged, opened it again. Bill wanted to make sure he could get in and out as he pleased!

Lucy-Ann flew to Jack and hugged him tightly, tears pouring down her face. Dinah grinned at Bill, and tried hard to stop herself hugging him. But she couldn't. She too was so relieved at seeing them both.

'No time to waste,' said Bill. 'Where's Philip?'

'Oh, Bill, he's gone!' said Lucy-Ann, turning to him and clinging to his arm. 'When we got down here tonight he was gone! And we don't know where or how. We don't know if the men caught him, or if Philip went off by himself, or what. He didn't leave a note or anything. But we think maybe he explored that secret way under the tapestry.'

'Bill, the men are coming back soon,' said Dinah, suddenly remembering. 'I heard one of them say to another, in English, that they were to have their last meeting here tonight. So they may be back here any time, because this is where they meet, and where they keep their maps, or whatever it is they look at so carefully.'

'Where are the maps?' asked Bill at once, and Dinah nodded towards the locked drawers.

'In there. But they keep them locked up. Bill, what are you going to do? Isn't this a mystery?'

'I'm beginning to see daylight,' said Bill grimly. 'Now look here, Dinah – you and Lucy-Ann are to go with Tassie straight away down the hill to Spring Cottage, and you are to stay there till we come. Do you understand? You can go out of that side door in the wall, which is now open. The man I have left upstairs will take you there safely and see you out. Then you must go at once.'

'But—but . . .' began Dinah, not liking to go without Philip.

'No buts,' said Bill. 'I'm in command here, and you do exactly as you're told! Now – off you go! We'll be with you tomorrow!'

Dinah, Lucy-Ann and Tassie went obediently up the steps and out of the entrance hole. The man at the top went off to the door in the wall with them, and saw them safely out on the hillside. 'Sure you know your way?' he murmured, for he was quite sure *he* wouldn't know his way down the dark hillside! But Tassie did. She could almost have found her way with her eyes shut, she knew it so well, and was so sure footed.

The girls disappeared into the night. The man returned to his post. The entrance to the secret room was now closed. Below, Bill, Jack and the others were hurriedly getting into the suits of armour. Bill meant to attend the next meeting of Scar-Neck with his men! Jack was glad to see that they all had revolvers! The men said very little. They were the least talkative people the boy had ever known.

Jack was made to stand in the suit of armour right at the back of the hidden room. Bill didn't want him too near, in case, as he said, there was a really rough house! The boy was shaking with excitement.

Kiki was not down in the room. Tassie had carried her firmly up the stone steps, screeching with annoyance at being parted from Jack so soon again. But it would not be possible to have a talkative parrot down there – she would certainly give the game away.

But Button the fox cub was there! Nobody knew it, of course. The fox cub had curled himself up under the bed, where Philip had hidden, glad to smell the familiar smell of the master he loved. Jack had forgotten all about him.

Soon all the suits of armour were standing once more on their pedestals round the curious museum-like room. Only three of them were empty. All the others were filled, though one of the men, a great big fellow, complained bitterly that his didn't fit him at all.

'Now – silence,' said Bill. 'Not a word from anyone. I think I heard something!'

27

The adventure boils up

But it was not anyone – it was a peal of thunder so loud that the noise had penetrated even down to the underground room.

'I hope the girls won't be frightened,' said Bill, thinking of them scurrying down the hillside in the darkness. 'I wonder if it's raining.'

'They'll be all right with Tassie, I think,' said Jack. 'She will know places to shelter in. She won't be silly enough to stand under trees or anything like that. There are a few little caves here and there in the hillside. Maybe they'll use those till the storm is past.'

Silence again. It was astonishing how so many people, all standing rather uncomfortably in suits of armour, could manage to do so without a single creak or clank!

One man cleared his throat, and the sound was strange in the hidden room.

'Don't do that again, Jim,' said Bill. There was dead silence once more. Jack sighed softly. It was unbearably exciting to stand hidden in armour, wet with perspiration, almost panting with heat, waiting for the other men to come.

Then suddenly, sounding quite loud, there came the noise of a door being unlocked. Then the tapestry on one wall shook – and someone lifted it up from behind!

Everyone stiffened inside the suits of armour. Eyes peered through the visors. Who was coming?

A man came out from behind the tapestry, and folded it back, hanging one end on a nail, so that others following could come into the room easily. Jack saw an opening behind, leading into the wall. From it came soft-footed men, one after the other – and with them they brought Philip!

The shaggy-browed man came first. Then came the bearded man, the one Bill called Scar-Neck, dragging Philip. Scar-Neck had the neck of his shirt closed, and Jack could see no sign of the tell-tale scar.

Philip was putting on a bold face, but Jack knew he was feeling scared. After him came three more men, all ugly fellows, with sharp eyes and stern mouths. They came into the room, talking. They left the secret way open, and Jack wondered where it led to.

Philip's hands were bound behind his back, so tightly that the rope bit into his skin. Scar-Neck flung him into a chair.

It was soon clear that Philip had only just been captured. Scar-Neck rounded on him almost at once.

'How long have you been in the castle? What do you know?'

'I was here with the girls,' said Philip. 'I hid under the bed. You never looked there. I wasn't doing any harm. We only came to play about in this old castle. We didn't know it belonged to anyone.'

'Get the girls,' growled Scar-Neck to the shaggy man. 'Bring them over here. We'll cross-question the whole three of them. To think that a parcel of kids should waste our time like this!'

The shaggy-browed man went over to the bed, where, he imagined, the two girls would, as usual, be sleeping. But when he pulled back the curtain, they were not there! He stared, and then roughly pulled off the blankets and rugs.

'They're not here!' he said, in an astonished voice. The bearded man turned at once.

'Don't be a fool! They must be here somewhere! We know they can't get out of this room once it's shut.'

'The boy may have let them out from above,' said the shaggy man. Scar-Neck swung round on Philip. The boy was amazed that the girls had gone, but he was not going to show it.

The shaggy man hunted under the bed – but it was plain to everyone that the girls had gone. Scar-Neck spoke roughly to Philip.

'Did you let them out?'

'No,' said Philip. 'I didn't. I was hiding here, I tell you, under the bed. I wasn't at the top.'

'Well – who let them out, then?' said the shaggy man, and his brows knitted together so that they almost hid his sharp eyes.

'Now – you tell us everything!' said Scar-Neck, and his voice was suddenly ugly and threatening.

Philip said nothing, but stared defiantly at the man. Scar-Neck lost his temper, raised his fist, and gave Philip such a blow on the side of the head that the boy fell off his chair. He picked himself up.

Jack, beside himself with anger, saw Philip's left ear glow bright scarlet, and begin to swell.

'Now will you talk?' said Scar-Neck, his voice growing with rage. The others looked on, saying nothing.

Still Philip said nothing. Jack felt proud. How brave he was! Then, to his horror, the man took out a revolver and laid it on the table beside him.

'We have ways of making sulky boys talk,' he said, and his eyes gleamed with rage.

Philip didn't like the look of the shining weapon. He blinked a little, and then stared at Scar-Neck again. But still he said nothing.

What would have happened next if there hadn't been a sudden and surprising interruption, nobody knew! But all at once, like a stone from a catapult, Button, who had slunk under a chair on the far side of the room when the men arrived, shot out and threw himself on Philip.

Everyone leapt to his feet, and Scar-Neck caught up his revolver. When they saw that the newcomer was only a fox cub, they sat down again, feeling angry at their sudden fright.

Scar-Neck was furious. He lashed out at the cub, and sent him rolling to the ground. Button bared his small white teeth.

'Don't hurt him,' said Philip, in alarm. 'He's only a cub. He's mine.'

'How did he get down here? When the girls got out, I suppose?' growled the shaggy man.

'I don't know,' said Philip, puzzled. 'I tell you, I really don't know how the girls got out, nor how the cub got in. It's as much a mystery to me as to you.'

'If this kid is telling the truth, we'd better finish up and get going,' said the shaggy man, sounding rather anxious. 'There must be others about, though goodness knows we've kept a good enough watch. Let's settle up our business and go.'

A rumble of thunder came down into the secret room again. The men looked at one another uneasily.

'What's that?' said the shaggy man.

'Thunder, of course,' growled Scar-Neck. 'What's the matter with you? Getting nervy just because a bunch of silly kids are playing around? What they want is a good beating, and I'll see this boy gets it before we go, anyway, even if those girls have gone!'

Button curled up quietly at Philip's feet. He was afraid of these men. Scar-Neck nodded to one of the others, and he got up. He went to the drawer where the documents were kept, unlocked it, and drew out the sheaf of papers there. He put them in front of Scar-Neck.

Then began a long discussion in a language that Philip did not understand. But Bill understood it! Bill could speak eight or more different languages, and he listened eagerly to all that was said.

Philip sat listlessly on his chair, his wrists hurting him, and his left ear now twice its size. He could not even rub it because his hands were so tightly tied behind his back.

Button licked his bare leg. It was comforting. Philip wondered where the girls had gone. How had they got out? He was glad to know they had probably escaped. Had help come? Had Jack managed to find someone? Would they rescue him too?

He wished he was standing safely inside the suit of armour he had hidden in before. He glanced round at it, and then stared in the utmost amazement.

Surely eyes were gleaming behind that visor? Philip had extremely good eyesight, and it so happened that the rays of the lamp shone directly into the visor of the armour he was looking at. It seemed to Philip as if there were real eyes behind it, not the usual hollow space.

He glanced at the next suit of armour, and saw what he imagined were eyes there too – and the next one! He felt terribly scared. Had all these suits of armour come alive all of a sudden? Who was inside? He could see that most of them were filled. He began to tremble.

Scar-Neck noticed him and laughed. 'Ah, so you are beginning to be afraid of what may happen to boys who interfere in somebody else's business! Maybe you will talk soon!'

Philip said nothing. He began to think clearly, and it was soon plain to him that it must be friends inside the armour, and not enemies. How silly of him to be scared! But it really had been an eerie feeling to see gleaming eyes looking at him from behind those visors.

'So that's how it is the girls have gone,' he thought. 'Now I understand. Jack did get help – and they've had the idea of doing what I did – hiding in the armour to see what is happening! Well, I mustn't give them away, whatever happens! I wonder if one of them is old Freckles.'

Feeling very much better now, the boy gave another look round at the armour. He did not dare to stare too hard, in case one of the men followed the direction of his look and saw what he saw.

Another rumble of thunder came down into the room, louder this time. The air was almost unbearably hot down there, and the men in the armour had hard work not to gasp. Perspiration ran down their bodies, and they longed to shift their positions a little. But they dared not move.

Bill was listening intently to all that was being said, though Philip could not make out a single word. Papers were spread out on the table, but Bill could not see what they were. They looked like blueprints of some sort, details of machinery perhaps. It was impossible for him to see.

Scar-Neck rolled them up at last. Then he turned to Philip.

'Well, our job is done. We shall not have the pleasure of seeing you or your friends any more. But before we go we shall teach you what it means to spy on us! Where's that rope?'

'Don't you dare touch me!' cried Philip, jumping to his feet. Scar-Neck took the rope.

Then, to his unutterable horror, one of the suits of armour walked off its pedestal, held up a stiff and clanking arm, at the end of which shone a wicked-looking revolver, and said:

'The game's up, Scar-Neck. We've got you all!'

The voice sounded hollow. Scar-Neck and the others stared in the utmost dismay, and then looked round at other suits of armour, which were also coming alive! It seemed like a bad dream – but a dream that had too many revolvers in it!

'Hands up!' said Bill's sharp voice.

Scar-Neck began to put his hands up – but suddenly he turned, took hold of the oil lamp, and smashed it on the ground. In a moment the room was pitch dark!

28

A terrible storm

Bill gave a cry of rage. Then Jack heard his voice. 'Get under the bed, Jack and Philip, quick! There may be shooting!'

The boys did exactly as they were told. They dived for the bed, Jack clanking in his armour. Philip lay there panting, wishing his hands were not tied. Jack got stuck halfway under the bed.

What was happening in the room they didn't know. There were shouts and panting and groans – but nobody did any shooting. It was too dark to risk that in case friend shot friend. It sounded to the boys as if men in armour and men without were rolling on the ground together, for there was a tremendous thudding and clashing.

Suddenly there was a grating noise, and the boys knew the entrance above was being opened. But who was opening it, their side or the other? Philip had no idea how it was opened from below, though he had often tried to find out, for obviously there must be a way.

Then he knew that Scar-Neck or one of his friends must have opened it, as a way of escape, for he heard Bill's voice shouting up to the man he had left above.

'Tom! Look out! Shoot anyone coming up!'

Tom sprang to the top of the steps, but he could see nothing down below. He could only hear the groans and clanks the boys could hear. Then up the steps crept one of the men. Tom did not hear him, and suddenly he felt a blow that sent him sprawling. It was Scar-Neck trying to escape. In the fight he had lost his revolver or he would certainly have shot Tom.

Before Tom could get up and catch him, he was gone –

and yet another man was on top of the surprised Tom, falling over him. Poor Tom got another blow, and his head sang. Then the shaggy-browed man kicked him savagely and disappeared too.

After that Tom didn't know what to do – whether to stand at the top of the steps to prevent anyone else coming up, or to go after the escaping men. But as he hadn't the remotest idea where they had gone, he chose the first course.

Down below things were going badly for the three men left. One of them was completely knocked out. Another had given in because Bill had sat on top of him so firmly that there wasn't anything else to do. And the third man had tried to escape down the secret way behind the tapestry, but was now being forcibly brought back by Jim, who was yanking him along with many muttered threats.

Bill at last found a torch and switched it on. The oil lamp was smashed beyond repair. It was fortunate that it had not set the place on fire. By the light of the powerful torch Bill had a look round.

The man he had been sitting on was now in the charge of someone else, and was looking extremely sorry for himself. He had a black eye and a very large lump on his head. Bill looked odd. He was still wearing his armour, but he had taken off the helmet so that his bald head, with the thick hair at each side, rose up startlingly.

The two boys came out from under the bed. Bill had to tug at Jack to set him free. Jack got out of the hot armour as quickly as he could, and freed Philip's hands.

Bill's face wore a look of utter disgust. He could see that the two men he most wanted to catch – Scar-Neck and the shaggy-browed man – were gone. He called up to Tom.

'Are you there, Tom?'

'Yes, sir,' came back Tom's voice, rather subdued.

'Have you got the two who came up the steps?' shouted Bill.

'No, sir. Sorry to say they bowled me over and got away, sir,' replied Tom, even more subdued.

Bill muttered a few rude names for the unlucky Tom. 'Come on down here,' he said. 'What a fool you are, Tom! You had a wonderful position up there – you could have stopped a whole army getting out!'

'Well, it was so dark, sir,' said Tom. 'I couldn't see a thing.'

'Well, you've let two of our most important men go,' said Bill grimly. 'That's not the way to get promotion, you know. I wish I'd put someone else up there now. I suppose those fellows are well away down the hill now. I've no doubt they've got their own powerful car well hidden away somewhere, ready for an emergency, and will be the other side of the country by tomorrow night.'

Poor Tom looked very sheepish. He was an enormous fellow, and the boys thought he ought to have been able to capture two enemies single-handed! They were in a terrible state of excitement and wished that they had been able to capture Scar-Neck themselves.

'Tie up these fellows,' said Bill, curtly nodding to their captives. Jim began to do it very efficiently and soon the men sat like trussed fowls, sullen and tousled, frowning into space.

'Now we'll have a look at those papers,' said Bill, and one of his men went to spread them out before him. Bill bent over them.

'Yes – they've got everything here they wanted to know,' he said. 'That fellow Scar-Neck is about the cleverest spy in any country. I bet he felt mad to leave these behind. They are worth a fortune to him, and are of untold value to the country he was spying for.'

One of the men rolled them up. As he did so a terrific roll of thunder echoed all round. Everyone looked startled.

'What a storm!' said the man called Jim. 'Was that lightning then?'

It was, flashing down even to the underground room. It had flashed almost at the same moment as the thunder crashed.

'Storm's about overhead, I should think,' said Bill. 'I don't think we'll venture down the hillside ourselves till it's over.'

'Aren't you going to see where that secret way leads to?' asked Jack, in disappointment.

'Oh yes,' said Bill. 'Tom and I will go, whilst the others take the prisoners down the hill – but we'll wait till daylight now, I think.'

The storm grew worse. Philip tried to tell Bill what had happened to him that day, but he had to shout at the top of his voice, because the thunder crashed so loudly overhead.

'I was so bored I thought I'd go down the secret passage myself and see where it led to,' shouted Philip. 'So when the men had gone up the stone steps after a good long sleep here, I slipped out from under the bed and went into that hole in the wall there. The men had left it open, just as you see it now, with the tapestry hooked back, and the stone slid from the opening. It goes right back, as you can see. Well, there's a door in the side of the opening. . . .'

The thunder interrupted him again and he stopped. Everyone was listening to him with interest, except the surly prisoners.

'The door there was locked, but someone had left the key in the lock,' went on Philip, when the thunder had died down a little. 'So I unlocked it. The door pushed backwards and I found myself in a narrow passage.'

'Wasn't it dark?' asked Jack.

'Yes, but I had my torch,' said Philip. 'I put it on, and saw my way quite well. The passage went downwards, at first between walls of stone – must have been the foundations of the castle, I suppose – and then I saw that I must have come out from under the castle, and was going through a tunnel hewn out of the solid rock.'

'And I suppose it led you out on to the hill on the other side?' said Bill. 'And you looked down on something rather interesting?'

'I never got as far as that,' said Philip. 'I heard one of the men coming some way behind me, and I thought I'd better hide. So I climbed up on to a narrow ledge near the roof of the passage just there, and lay quite quiet.'

'Golly!' said Jack. 'Did he pass you?'

'Yes. But he was looking for me,' said Philip. 'You see, I'd forgotten to close the door that led into the secret passage, and when the men came back, they noticed it, and got puzzled. So they sent someone down the passage to see who had opened the door.'

'And they found you?' said Bill, but his words were lost in another crash of thunder.

'When the man found I wasn't anywhere in the passage he came back,' went on Philip. 'But evidently the chief man wasn't going to let me wander about there, and he and everyone else came down the secret way then. And, of course, they soon found me lying on that narrow ledge, and dragged me down.'

'What happened to you then?' asked Bill. 'You weren't taken back to the hidden room, because the girls wondered where you were when they came down that night.'

'No. They tied my wrists together, and my ankles too, and just left me there in the passage,' said Philip. 'They said as I seemed to have a liking for the passage, I could stay there till they were ready to bring me back and question me. So there I stayed till at last they did fetch me. They untied my ankles so that I could walk – and brought me to the hidden room, as you saw.'

'Poor old Philip – a nasty experience,' said Bill.

'Golly, I *was* scared when I saw your eyes gleaming at me through the visor of the helmet, Bill,' said Philip. 'I had the fright of my life! But I soon realised you must be friends.'

The thunder was now so noisy and continuous that it was no use talking. They all sat in silence, thinking what a tremendous storm must be going on outside on the hill.

'I'm just going up to have a squint out of the front door,' said Bill. 'It must be a fine sight, this storm.'

'We'll come too,' said the boys. So up the stone steps they went, and down the hall to the open front door of the castle.

They stopped in awe just before they got there. The whole countryside lay cowering beneath the worst storm they had ever seen. Lightning tore the sky apart continually, great jagged forks that ran up and down from the top of the sky to the bottom.

The thunder was like nothing they had ever heard, it was loud and so overwhelming. It never stopped! It rolled round and round the hillside, like terrific guns bombarding an enemy.

And the rain! It poured down as if great rivers had been let loose from the sky. No one could go out in that, for they would surely be battered to the ground!

'It's a cloud burst,' said Bill. 'The sky has opened, and let down a deluge! I've never seen anything like this, except once in India. I should think Scar-Neck and the other fellow are having a pretty bad time of it out on the hillside.'

'Anyway the girls had plenty of time to get down to Spring Cottage,' said Jack. 'They'll be safe at home, I hope. Good gracious – what's that?'

29

The secret passage

As Jack was speaking, there came the most tremendous clap of thunder he was ever to hear in his life. It made him jump violently and cling to Bill. It was the loudest noise he had ever heard.

With it came a flash of lightning that lighted up the hills around for miles upon miles. There they were, unbelievably clear and somehow unreal, for half a second. Then they went back into pitch darkness again. But a queer feeling ran through all three when the flash came.

Bill suddenly pulled them back a little. 'I think the castle has been struck!' he said. 'Yes, it has – look!'

One of the towers, lit up by the next flash, was seen by the two boys to be in the act of falling! In a second it was gone as darkness came back again. Then, through the insistent thudding of the rain, came the sound of the crashing of stone upon stone, as the tower fell to the ground.

'The storm is absolutely on top of us!' shouted Jack. 'Let's go back to the hidden room, Bill. I'm afraid. I felt that flash of lightning, I'm sure I did. Bill, the thunder is in the courtyard, it is, it is!'

Bill was almost inclined to believe that it was, as it rolled round in rumbling crashes. Then another flash came, and once more the three felt a queer shock, as the lightning seemed to flash through them.

'I believe if we hadn't got rubber-soled shoes on we'd have been struck dead!' thought Bill suddenly. 'Gosh, the castle has been struck again – this time the main building. It will be in ruins if this goes on!'

He hustled the boys back to the steps that led to the

hidden room. Down they went, and then paused in awe – for now it seemed as if the castle itself was falling!

Hurriedly Bill pulled at the spike that shut the entrance. He felt he would like to have solid stone between him and the storm now. With relief he saw the stone slide sideways and upwards, and the entrance was closed.

Almost immediately there came a terrific sound of falling stone, crashing on to stone below, and the room shook.

'The castle is falling on top of us!' cried Philip,and he went pale. It really sounded as if it was. Bill thought part of it must again have been struck by lightning, and have fallen inwards. He wondered if what they heard was the floor above falling down into the hall! It sounded like that.

More crashing noises came, not made by the thunder, and then comparative silence. No one spoke for a while.

'I can see how that landslide happened,' said Bill at last. 'A storm like this could easily cause undermining of the road, and a landslide would result. I shouldn't be surprised if there was another one tonight. I should think even more of the road will be destroyed.'

'That rain was so terrific,' said Jack. 'I've never heard anything like it. I bet the poor girls are scared, down in the cottage by themselves.'

'Yes – I wish we were with them,' said Bill. He took a glance at the captives. They looked very frightened. What they could hear of the storm and the falling of the castle was evidently filling them with forebodings as to what might be going to happen next!

'You know, I've just realised that I'm awfully hungry,' said Philip suddenly. 'I've had nothing to eat since I went off by myself to explore that secret passage.'

'You must be famished!' said Bill. 'I feel pretty hungry myself too. There seems to be a nice pile of tins over there. I think it might while away the time a bit, and make us forget this awful storm, if we attacked the contents.'

Jack and Philip examined the tins. They chose one tin of spiced meat, one tin of tongue and two of peaches. They opened them, and put generous helpings on to the plates stacked on a side table.

Bill found drinks. It was so hot that the beer he found in bottles was more than usually welcome to the men. The boys feasted on ginger beer and lemonade, both of which were there too.

Everyone felt better after the meal. The storm seemed to be dying down. Bill glanced at his watch.

'Half-past five!' he said, with a yawn. 'I didn't think it was so late. Well, as the storm is dying, maybe we could get out into the courtyard for a breath of air. It will be daylight now. I can perhaps see my men off down the hillside with their prisoners.'

'Yes. I'm dying for a breath of air,' said Philip, whose face was bright scarlet with heat. 'How do you open the entrance, from down here, Bill?'

'Up there by the ceiling,' said Bill, and showed Philip how. There was a hidden lever there. He pulled at it – but it did not move. He pulled again.

'It won't budge,' said Bill, surprised. 'Here, Tom, you try. You're as strong as a horse.'

Tom took his turn, but he could not move the lever either. The stone would not move an inch from the entrance, to unblock it.

Then both Bill and Tom tried together. The stone moved an inch or two – and then stopped. No further efforts made any difference. It wouldn't move any more.

Bill went up the steps as far as he could and tried to peer through the crack, but he could see nothing at all. He came back.

'I'm afraid part of the castle has fallen in on top of the entrance,' he said. 'The lever is strong enough to move that heavy stone, but we are not strong enough to shift whatever is on top of it by pulling hard. We can't get out.'

'We'll have to use the other way then, the passage I went down yesterday,' said Philip, nodding his head towards the opening behind the tapestry.

'Yes,' said Bill. 'I only hope that hasn't done any slipping and sliding too! Still, you said it was made out of the solid rock, didn't you? It should be quite all right.'

It was steadily getting hotter and hotter in the underground room. Button, who had retired under the bed during the fight, now came out and rolled over on his side by Philip, his pink tongue hanging out like a dog's.

'He's thirsty,' said Jack. 'Give him a drink.'

'There's nothing except ginger beer left,' said Philip, and poured some out on a plate. Button was so thirsty that he drank it all up, then sat down and licked his mouth round thoughtfully, as if to say, 'Well – that was certainly nice and wet – but what a strange taste!'

'We shall all be cooked if we don't make a move,' said Bill. 'Come on – we'll try our luck this way. I'll go first.'

He went into the hole in the wall, and pushed at the door there. It opened. Bill went through, shining his torch in front of him.

The two boys followed. Then came the three men with their captives, who were now very subdued indeed. They had not uttered a word for a very long time.

The passage was narrow, but fairly straight at first. Bill's torch showed that it was built in the stone foundations of the castle itself.

'It's likely that there are dungeons built down here too,' said Bill. 'It's a strange old place. There are probably more hidden rooms as well. The old legends about the place talk of more than one room.'

After a while the stone of the tunnel walls turned to solid

rock, uneven of surface. The air was surprisingly fresh. It was deliciously cool after the oven-heat of the room they had left behind.

Now the passage wound about a little, as if to follow the vagaries of the rock. Bill thought part of the passage was artificial, and part natural. It was plain that it went straight through the top of the hill, in a downward direction.

In some places it sloped quite steeply, and they all slithered a little. Then they suddenly heard the noise of water!

They stopped. Bill looked back at Philip. 'Water!' he said. 'Did you see any before when you came down here?'

Philip shook his head. 'No,' he said. 'It was all quite dry. We haven't yet come to the ledge I hid on.'

They went on, puzzled – and suddenly they saw what made the noise! The deluge of rain soaking down into the hillside was trying to get away somewhere, and was running down in a torrent, underground. It had found a weak place in the wall of the passage, and had poured down into it. It was now running like a river down the tunnel, making a roaring, gurgling noise.

'Goodness!' said Jack, peering over Bill's shoulder, and seeing the rushing water by the light of his torch. 'We can't go down there now!'

'It's not very deep,' said Bill, looking at it. 'I believe we shall be able to wade along all right. It's lucky for us that the passage goes downhill, not uphill, or we should have had the water pouring to meet us!'

He put his foot into it, and found that it was about knee-deep. The current was fairly powerful, but not enough to sweep anyone from their feet, though they had to take care to keep their balance.

They all waded into the torrent. It was cold and the coolness was welcome to them. Splashing through the water they went on their way again. Button was curled tightly round Philip's neck. He hated the water.

They went on a good way. Then Philip pointed up to a rocky ledge near the roof of the passage. 'That's where I hid,' he said. 'See? It was quite a good place, wasn't it? Nobody would have found me if they hadn't really been looking for me.'

They went on past Philip's ledge. The water was a little deeper now, and stronger, because the passage sloped more steeply just there. It was slow going. Jack, who was getting very tired, thought it would never come to an end. He liked adventures, but he began to feel he would rather like a rest from this one.

All at once the passage began to slope down very steeply indeed, so steeply that the torrent made quite a waterfall! Bill stopped.

'Well, I don't see how we can get down here, unless we just slide down in the water!' he said. 'Ah, but wait a minute – I believe there are stone steps leading downwards. Yes, there are. We shall be all right if we don't let the water rush us off our feet!'

He went first, very cautiously, feeling for the steps with his feet. The boys followed, equally cautiously, Jack almost being rushed off his feet once or twice by the surging fall of water.

Suddenly Bill put his torch out – and daylight appeared in front! The stone steps led out on to the opposite side of the castle hill – they were there at last!

Bill leapt out of the water and came out of a narrow opening in the hillside, almost completely covered by brambles. 'Well – here we are!' he said. 'Safe after all!'

30

The other side of the hill

The boys came out of the hole too, and they all stared at the sight below them. They were on a very steep hillside, with an almost sheer drop beneath.

Directly below was what looked like a farmhouse, with out-buildings on the slope of the hill. All around the place was barbed wire, rows upon rows of it. There was plenty just below where they stood, too.

There was a copse of trees behind the house, and in the middle was a clear space. A curious looking machine stood in the centre of this clearing. It was large and shining. To anyone down at the farm or near by it must have been completely hidden in the trees – but viewed from above it was very plain to see.

'What is it?' asked Jack, gazing at it in the clear morning sunlight.

'Not even I know that, Jack,' said Bill. 'It is one of our own country's secrets – something being worked on by our greatest military scientists.'

'And that's what Scar-Neck the spy was after?' asked Philip.

'That's what he was after,' said Bill. 'He got wind of it – found out where the tests were being carried out in secret – and discovered to his delight that there was an old castle on the other side of the hill for sale.'

'Gosh! Did he buy the castle then?' asked Jack.

Bill nodded. 'Yes. I made it my business to find out who the owner was. Scar-Neck had not bought it in his own name, or course – he was far too clever for that. He bought it in the name of an Englishman – called Brown. A man supposed to be interested in old buildings. But I soon found out who was behind Brown.'

'Aren't you clever, Bill?' said Jack admiringly.

'No,' said Bill. 'That kind of thing is easy in my job. I knew Scar-Neck was probably after this secret of ours, but I couldn't for the life of me see how he could find out anything. As you can see, it's very well hidden up here at the back of the old farm – and well protected by barbed wire, which is quite probably mixed up with other wire that is electrically charged.'

'Well – how did he get the secret then?' said Philip.

'By wonderful photography, and by making a way right under the wire down to the machine itself, I imagine,' said Bill. 'Look – do you see signs of digging there? Well, I imagine Scar-Neck and his friends did a bit of burrowing, like rabbits, right under the wire, and came up safely inside the enclosure.'

'Wouldn't anyone see them?' said Jack.

'Not from this side,' said Bill. 'Nobody would guess anyone would try any tricks from up here. It would seem impossible to get here, it's so steep!'

'And nobody knew about the passage in the castle that led right to this side of the hill!' said Jack. 'How did he find it out?'

'Got old plans of the castle, I expect,' said Bill. 'The old fellow who had this castle last was quite mad, as you no doubt gathered from the curious things he did. He made all kinds of hidden rooms with curious contrivances, and lived in a romantic world of his own. Scar-Neck found the hidden room we know extremely useful, and the secret passage a perfect godsend! It actually came out above the very secret he had been sent to find out!'

'He's a brave man,' said Philip.

'Yes – most spies are brave,' said Bill. 'But this particular one is a most unpleasant fellow, heartily disliked even in his own country. He will double-cross anyone, not excepting his dearest friend. Well – I'm afraid he's got away this time. But thank goodness he's left the plans of our secret behind him in that hidden room!'

'So he can't do any damage, I suppose?' asked Philip.

'Not unless he remembers everything in his head,' said Bill. 'He has a marvellous memory, of course, so maybe he will do us some damage even now.'

'I hope he won't,' said Philip. 'I do so wish we had caught him, Bill – and old Shaggy too. I didn't like either of them at all.'

'These three we have got are only ordinary toughs, ready to do anything beastly for money,' said Bill. 'I have let the real culprits slip – and I shall get a rap over the knuckles for that! Serves me right – I had a wonderful chance of catching them. I should have guessed that Scar-Neck might smash that lamp.'

Everyone had been glad of the rest and fresh air. Now Bill got up and looked down hill. How could they get down without being torn to bits by the barbed wire? No one felt inclined to wriggle down the tunnel Scar-Neck had made below it.

Bill saw someone about below. He gave a hail, and the man looked up, evidently overcome with surprise to see so many people standing high up on the hillside.

'Who are you?' he yelled.

'Friends!' shouted back Bill. 'Is Colonel Yarmouth there? I know him, and would like to talk to him. But I can't get through this wire.'

'Look!' said Jack suddenly, and pointed to a beautiful camera standing under a thick bramble. 'That's how they got their pictures! With that! It's one of the finest cameras I've ever seen. It hasn't been hurt by the deluge either – it's got a waterproof protection. I expect that camera you gave me is ruined now, Bill. It was in the gorse bush and had no protection at all. I left it there, unfortunately.'

'What a pity!' said Bill. 'Well – maybe I can arrange for you to have this one instead – as a little return for letting me in on your adventure, Jack!'

Jack's eyes gleamed. What pictures he could take if he had a camera like that! It must be one of the finest in the world.

Another man now came out in the grounds at the back of the farm-house below. Jack had expected a colonel to be in uniform, but he wasn't.

'Hi, Yarmouth!' yelled Bill. 'Don't you know me?'

'Well, I'm blessed!' floated up the Colonel's astonished voice. 'I'll send a couple of men up to make a way down for you.'

So, in a fairly short time, a way was made for them through the rows of barbed wire which was promptly repaired again behind them. They went down to the farm-house, slithering and almost falling down the steep descent.

The Colonel and Bill disappeared into the house, to talk. The others waited patiently outside. Jack and Philip lay down on the heather and yawned. They both fell asleep at once!

After a while the Colonel and Bill came out and snapped out a few orders. Three of his men took away the captives and they were put into a whitewashed room near by, which looked as if it had once been a dairy. The door was shut and padlocked.

'That's got rid of *them*!' said Bill, pleased. 'Now we'll get back to Spring Cottage. I'm afraid we'll have to go down to the bottom of the hill, take the road there, and then make our way up the other side to the cottage. There is apparently no other way to get there.'

The boys, awake now, groaned. They really didn't feel like any more walking. Still, it had to be done.

'What about the maps, or whatever they were, we left behind in the hidden room?' asked Jack.

'Oh, we can easily get those. One of the Colonel's men will go up through that passage and get them as soon as the water has stopped,' said Bill. 'And the three prisoners will be sent down sometime today under guard, to be dealt with later.'

'I suppose the adventure is over?' said Philip. 'Quite finished?'

'Well – there are a few loose ends to tie up,' said Bill. 'We must just see if we can find any trace of Scar-Neck and his friend in any of the districts near at hand. Scar-Neck will probably cut off his fine beard – but if he does that he shows his scar, unless he can paint it out. We may get on his track again and catch him. That would really be a most satisfactory finish, wouldn't it!'

'We'll have to go and get your car too, won't we?' said Jack, remembering. 'We left it at the beginning of the landslide.'

'So we did,' said Bill. 'My word, I hope it hasn't been swept away by that deluge of rain – or buried in another landslide!'

'I want to know what happened to the girls too,' said Philip. 'I'm hoping they all got back safely before the storm really started. It seems ages since I've seen them!'

They went on down the hillside, guided by a man from the farmhouse. He was extremely interested in their adventures, but wasn't told much beyond that they had got caught in the castle in the storm, and had had to find their way through an old passage.

Button was now running at Philip's heels, happy to be in the open air. Even he had played his part in the adventure, for he had shown Tassie how to get in and out of the castle without using doors, gates or windows!

They came to the bottom of the hill and took the road there. Then they came to the lane that led up to Spring Cottage.

'There it is at last!' cried Jack, and sprinted up to it. 'Hi, girls, here we are! Where are you?'

31

The end of the castle of adventure

There was a shriek from the cottage. It was Lucy-Ann of course. She came flying out of the door, her eyes shining, and flew straight at Jack. She almost bowled him over in her joy at seeing him again.

'Jack! You're back! And Philip! Wherever did you get to? We were awfully worried about you!'

Dinah and Tassie came running out too, exclaiming in pleasure. 'Were you all right in the storm? We got so worried about you! Tassie's been up the hill and she says half the castle has fallen down the hill!'

'Were *you* all right in that storm?' asked Jack, as they all went into the little house. 'We were very worried about you three girls having to go down the hill in that awful deluge! Did you get home before the storm really broke?'

'Well, the rain had begun, and there was thunder rolling round nearly all the time, but no lightning,' said Dinah. 'We were soaked by the time we got here. Tassie wouldn't let us rest for even a minute on the hill – she kept saying that there would be another landslide – and she was right!'

'Good old Tassie,' said Jack. 'She just got you back in time. I simply can't begin to tell you what it was like up in the castle!'

But he did tell them, of course, and they listened with their eyes wide open in horror. What a night!

'Where's Kiki?' asked Jack, looking all round. 'I thought she would be here to greet me.'

'She keeps flying off to look for you,' said Tassie. 'But she comes back. She won't be long, I'm sure.'

She wasn't. In about ten minutes' time she was back, sailing through the air, shouting loudly to Jack.

'How many times, how many times, how many times, fusty, musty, dusty, Jack, Jack, Jack!'

She flew to his shoulder and pecked his ear lovingly. Philip put up his hand to his left ear which was still swollen.

'Don't you fly on to *my* shoulder and peck *my* ear,' he said to Kiki. 'It's not ready for pecking or nibbling yet!'

The girls got breakfast for everyone, and talked nineteen to the dozen, happy at having the boys and Bill. Bill sent his three men up the road to find his car.

'And now,' said Bill, when they had finished eating, 'what about a sleep, boys? I'm tired out!'

Jack was almost asleep as it was, and Philip kept yawning. So the boys went up to sleep on their beds and Bill put himself on the couch in the kitchen. The girls went out into the garden to talk.

They had to put waterproofs down on the grass because it was so wet. The day was lovely now, with not a cloud to be seen. It was fresh and cool. The stormy heat had completely gone.

They lazed there, chattering, with Kiki joining in now and again. Button was asleep on Philip's middle upstairs. Kiki was not sleepy, so she did not go with Jack, but contented herself with taking a look at him now and again through the window, to make sure he was there.

'There's someone coming,' said Dinah suddenly. She sat up and looked.

'It's Bill's three men,' said Lucy-Ann, lazily.

The men came into the garden. They looked serious. 'Where's the Boss? We want him,' said one.

'He's asleep, so don't disturb him yet,' said Dinah.

'Sorry, missie, but I'm afraid we must disturb him,' said

the man. 'We've got news.'

'What news?' asked Lucy-Ann. 'Have you found the car?'

'Yes,' said the man. 'But we'll tell our news to the Boss, missie.'

'Well, he's in the kitchen,' said Dinah.

The men moved off to the kitchen. They woke Bill, and the three girls heard them telling him something in urgent, serious voices. Bill came out, and the girls looked enquiringly at him.

'What's up, Bill?' asked Dinah. 'Have they found your car – and is it smashed up, or something?'

'They've found my car all right,' said Bill, slowly. 'And they've found something else too.'

'What!' asked the three girls together.

'Well, apparently Scar-Neck and his friend went off over the landslide quite safely, and then found my car standing where we left it,' said Bill. 'They must have got into it and turned it round – and then the deluge struck them, and another landslide began!'

'Are they – killed?' asked Dinah.

'Well, I imagine so,' said Bill. 'We don't know. The landslide caught the car and took it along. It dumped it upside-down in a gully, where these men found it – with Scar-Neck and the other fellow inside.'

'Can't they get them out then?' asked Dinah, rather pale.

'The doors are jammed,' said Bill. 'Have you got a wire tow-rope, or any good strong rope that won't break? If you have, we'll take it and try to get the car the right way up. Then we may be able to open the roof and get the men out.'

Dinah fetched some wire rope from the shed. She gave it to Bill in silence. None of the girls asked to go with the men. This seemed a terrible ending, even to two bad men.

They waited impatiently for the boys to awake, and when at last they came down, yawning and complaining of feeling hungry again, the girls ran to tell them the news.

'Golly!' said Jack, startled. 'Fancy them finding the car like that! They must have thought it was a bit of luck. And then another landslide catches them – what a frightful shock they must have had!'

Bill came back some hours later. The children ran to meet him.

Bill was smiling. 'Neither of the men is dead,' he said. 'Scar-Neck has concussion and is quite unconscious and rather badly hurt. The other fellow has a broken leg, and was stunned too. But he's come round.'

'So you've captured them both after all!' said Philip. 'Well done, Bill!'

'What about the car?' asked Dinah.

'Looks wrecked to me,' said Bill. 'But I don't mind that. I reckon I shall be handed out a new car when my chief knows I've got Scar-Neck and his friend to pass over to him. It's quite a scoop for me – though I'd never have stumbled on to their secret if it hadn't been for you children!'

'Well, we'd have been in a pretty pickle if *you* hadn't turned up,' said Jack. 'Whatever will Aunt Allie say when she comes back and hears all that has happened since she has been gone?'

'She'll say she can't turn her back for a day or two without us all getting into mischief!' said Philip, with a grin. 'Where are the men, Bill?'

'I sent Tom down to the village for help, instead of taking him back to the car with me,' said Bill. 'And they sent up a couple of stretchers and a doctor who happened to be down there – so they will be on their way to hospital by now, I imagine – and when they wake up, they'll each find a nice burly policeman sitting by the side of their bed!'

'Oh, Bill – what an adventure!' said Dinah. 'I never dreamt we'd plunge into all this when we first came here – and it's all happened so quickly. I hope we shall have nice peaceful holidays for the rest of the time. I've had enough adventures to last me for a year!'

'I want to stretch my legs,' said Jack. 'What about walking up the hillside, Bill, and having a look to see what has happened to the castle?'

'Right,' said Bill, so they set off up the road to the castle. But they could not go nearly so far as usual, because the landslide had come a good deal farther down, and the hillside was a terrible, jumbled mass of wet rocks, heaps of soil, uprooted trees and running streams – a desolate-looking region, indeed.

'It's horrid,' said Lucy-Ann. Then she turned to gaze at the frowning castle, higher up. 'The castle looks different. Something's happened to it. Let's climb up and see.'

So they climbed up higher, taking the little rabbit path they always used. What a difference they found as they came near the castle!

'Two of the towers have gone, and most of the walls,' said Lucy-Ann, awed. 'We can walk right into the courtyard now, over the rubble of stones. What a noise they must have made when they fell!'

'And look at the castle! The middle part of it has fallen in! It's not much more than a shell now!' said Jack, staring.

It looked almost a ruin. Philip stared hard at it. 'The middle part must have crashed down into the big hall,' he said. 'No wonder you couldn't move that entrance stone, Bill. There must be tons of fallen boulders on top of it!'

Bill looked rather solemn. He could see what a narrow escape from death they had all had. If they had been anywhere else in the castle or courtyard they would have been crushed and buried. Being down in the hidden room had saved their lives!

'Good-bye to my camera and all our rugs and things,' said Jack.'

'I'll replace everything you have lost,' promised Bill, who, now that he had actually captured Scar-Neck, was ready to promise the whole world to anyone! 'And I'll give you all a fine present each for letting me share such a grand adventure!'

'Me too?' said Tassie, at once. She liked Bill.

'You too,' said Bill. 'What would you like, Tassie?'

'Three pairs of shoes all for myself,' said Tassie solemnly, and the others laughed. They knew Tassie wouldn't wear them. She would just keep them and love and admire them – but she would never wear them. Tassie didn't need to!

'Let's go back,' said Lucy-Ann. 'I don't want to look at that ruin any more.'

'Nor do I,' said Dinah, 'but somehow I feel as if it's better as a ruin, open to anyone who cares to explore it, than as a castle owned by wicked old men, or spies like Scar-Neck. I like it better now! I'm glad to think of those musty old rooms all buried away – they were horrid!'

'Fusty, musty, dusty!' sang Kiki, in delight. 'Pop goes the fusty, musty, dusty!'

'Idiot!' said Jack. 'You *will* always have the last word, won't you, Kiki?'

Then down the hill they went in the sunshine, leaving behind them the sad, broken old castle, its roof open to the wind and the rain, its proud towers fallen.

'The Castle of Adventure!' said Jack. 'You were right, Philip – it *was* the Castle of Adventure!'

Don't miss the next exciting book in Enid Blyton's thrilling Adventure series.

THE VALLEY OF ADVENTURE

Philip, Jack, Lucy-Ann, Dinah and Kiki have landed in a wild and beautiful valley by mistake . . .

'Now – round this next corner – and I bet we shall see the pass!' cried Jack. 'Then hurrah for the way out of this mysterious valley!'

They rounded the corner. Yes – there lay the pass – or what must once have been the pass. But it was a pass no longer.

Something had happened. The narrow way between the great mountains was blocked high with great rocks and black boulders. It was impassable.

At first the four children didn't quite take it in. They stood and stared in wonder.

'What's happened there?' said Jack at last. 'It looks like an earthquake or something. Did you ever see such a terrible mess?'

'Great holes have been blown in the rocky walls on either side of the pass,' said Philip.

They stared in silence, and then Jack turned to the others. 'Do you know what I think has happened?' he said. 'All that devastation has been caused by bombs – I'm sure it has.'